SUDDEN DEATH OVERTIME

by AL HAAS

GLASSSPIDERPUBLISHING

Cover design by Judith S. Design & Creativity
www.judithsdesign.com

Produced by Glass Spider Publishing
www.glassspiderpublishing.com

Author's Note

I want to thank my wife, Joanna Starr Hynes, for her help with this book. A veteran editor, she furnished research and editorial guidance and even came up with the title.

I'd also like to thank George Anastasia, a fellow *Philadelphia Inquirer* alum. A superb, organized crime reporter, George helped me understand the machinations of the Philadelphia mob.

Also, while this novel is largely imagined, there are occasions when the fiction intersects with fact. For example: Like the protagonist, I was in a patrol car that drove into the midst of a North Philadelphia gang fight punctuated by gunfire. Like the protagonist, I was treated to my tear gas baptism while covering an anti-war protest at Ft. Dix, N.J.

And like that main character, I was sitting at Philadelphia Police Commissioner Frank Rizzo's table during a press dinner when he told the rather physical story of how he dealt with a racist rabble-rouser.

(In the interest of not upsetting my family, I might emphasize that the sex scenes in this book are pure fiction.)

The celebrity anecdotes the protagonist recites for his friend were gleaned from my years as an *Inquirer* entertainment writer. The protagonist's Civil War dream was triggered by my great-grandfather's service in the war as a teenage member of the 5th Pennsylvania Cavalry, service that included getting two horses shot out from under him, according to my grandfather. He also told me that the second felled horse lay on his father for five hours and left him with a limp. (His cavalry saber and a copy of his enlistment certificate, the latter obtained from the National Archives, hang over my fireplace.)

With the notable exception of the North Philadelphia gang fight, which I set in 1969 but was based on a real experience that actually took place a bit later, the historical events mentioned in this novel occurred on the dates stated.

And yes, Virginia, there still is a John's Roast Pork at Snyder and Weccacoe in South Philadelphia. Ralph & Ricky's, another Philadelphia source of culinary truth and beauty mentioned in the book, is no longer located at Tasker and Taney, however. It moved to 7th and Oregon, where it remained until it closed in 2018. (I went there for a cheese steak, as I had for the 20 years I lived in South Philly, only to find it being remodeled for some other use. I felt gut-punched.)

PART ONE: 1969

DETROIT, MI

1969

For Ronald Harvick, a United Motors vice president, thoughts of murder were very recent intellectual guests. He had never contemplated killing anyone before, simply because it hadn't been necessary. None of the obstacles in the path of his corporate climb had proven insurmountable.

Indeed, it had all been so easy for so long.

Harvick started at United Motors in July 1940, shortly after receiving an engineering degree from Michigan State. His daydream about running the company soon metamorphosed into a goal. And because his 20/150 vision and punctured left ear drum made him immune to the draft when the U.S. entered World War II, the scansorial Harvick's ascendency at UM was uninterrupted.

Handsome, hardworking, and endowed with sensitive political antennae, he had left no promotional pathway untraveled. Night classes earned him an MBA. He had an appropriately preppy wife, and he and Mary were active in their community, as was expected of an executive and his mate. He was on the vestry of his Episcopal church in the posh Detroit suburb of Grosse Pointe Farms, and served as assistant scoutmaster of Grosse Pointe Farms Troop 29. Noticing that successful executives tended to be tall, Harvick wore elevator shoes that bumped up his 5-10 to an even six feet.

It all paid off. He quickly started jogging down the auto industry's answer to the tenure track. In 1952, at the age of only 34, he was named chief of drivetrain design for UM's Duryea Division, which built the company's volume car line.

By 1960, he was in Brussels, heading up engineering for the automaker's European vehicles. Seven years later, he had an office in UM's Detroit headquarters, just down the hall from the walnut-paneled corporate throne room occupied by Clifford R. Bowers, III, UM's chairman and president. The polished brass plate on Harvick's office door now read: Vice President—North American Operations.

When Bowers announced on January 29, 1969, that he would retire on May 1, Harvick had expected to get the job. At 51, after 29 years with the corporation, he was second in command and saw himself as the heir apparent.

March 3

Bowers announced his successor on this Monday morning. In a move that even surprised the chairman's main men, the board chose Kenneth Briggs, the 44-year-old wunderkind who, as UM's marketing chieftain, had dramatically ameliorated the sluggish sales of the corporation's bread and butter—the Duryea Division.

After the announcement, Harvick went into his office bathroom and threw up. Then, after staring sightlessly at his coat rack for ten minutes, he dialed a number his wife had given him for use in extraordinary circumstances.

No one at UM was aware of his connection to the man he called. Harvick didn't want his colleagues to know that his brother-in-law, the sibling of his supposedly waspy wife, was Antonio "Tony Tomato" Bonafucci, a culinary hobbyist and a made man in the Philadelphia mafia.

Harvick and his wife never mentioned Bonafucci, not even among themselves.

Bonafucci picked up his phone.

"Tony? This is Ron Harvick."

"Ron! To what do I owe this out-of-the-blue communication? You haven't talked to me since the wedding, and that was right after you got out of college, what, 30 years ago?"

"I had no choice, Tony. You know that."

"I saw that photo of you and my sister in *Time*," Bonafucci said then. "She was wearing a prim Presbyterian dress and that pale Protestant nail polish, so I suppose the deWOPification of your wife Mary, christened Maria Bonafucci, is now complete. But enough of that. What's on your mind, Ron? What do you want?"

"I want the death of Kenneth Briggs, UM's chairman-elect. I want his death to look like the result of a home invasion, and I want it to happen while Mary and I are in Hawaii on vacation. That will be from May 4 to 18."

"And why should I do this service for you?"

"Because when I then become the new chairman, and I will, there will be ways for UM to reward you and your organization."

There were five seconds of silence before Bonafucci responded. "Alright, I'll arrange it. I know a guy, outside my organization, that I occasionally use for out-of-town wet work. Think of him as a hit broker with a very skillful freelance crew. And he isn't cheap. To assign a hitter, he will need 10 large up front ($83,866 in 2023 dollars). I suggest you get pieces of that from several sources. One withdrawal the size of the hit fee could get noticed.

"Send me the money, and don't call me again," Bonafucci concluded. "I'll contact you when it's time to discuss my organization's business ties with yours."

"Okay."

MEMPHIS, TN
March 10
James Earl Ray pled guilty to killing the Rev. Dr. Martin Luther King, Jr.

PHILADELPHIA, PA

March 19

The voice on the phone was sodden with that synthetic collegiality that so often greases the gears of commerce. "Mako, old bean, how's it hangin'?"

"Good, Chief."

"Can you meet me in the garden, say around two? I have a little overtime for you."

"I'll be there. See you then."

At 2:00 p.m., the hit broker (addressed as "Chief" on the phone) sat down on a bench in the Philadelphia Museum of Art's Azalea Garden and waited for his top assassin. The March cold snap had ended abruptly on this sun-laved Wednesday, and the temperature now stood at 58 degrees. The zipper of his suede jacket remained at half-mast.

At 2:03, Mako took a seat next to him, and the two discussed what the killer would have to do to earn the "overtime" for taking out the United Motors chairman-elect.

Mako listened intently as Chief recited the ground rules for the job, absently tracing a long scar on his throat that nearly intersected the path of his right carotid artery.

"I can get it done within the time frame and make it look like a break-in," Mako said, finally. "I'll take out him and his wife, and grab some valuables so it looks like a robbery. By the way, what's this pay?"

"The usual: $7,500." ($59,555 in 2023 bucks.)

March 21

George Ennis, a 27-year-old newsman for the *Philadelphia Public Sentinel*, had spent this Friday night in North Philadelphia covering a five-alarm fire that had spread from a lumber yard to nearby houses.

Usually, a rewrite man like Ennis wouldn't have been out there on the edge of an inferno, listening to a harried battalion chief yelling at intense, adrenaline-fueled firemen. The *Public Sentinel*, like other big city dailies, did the bulk of its hard news gathering with a reporter/rewrite man tandem: The reporter, or district man, would cover the event, then unload his notes over the phone to a rewrite man who would compose the story. But when the night city editor, Denny Harrigan, found himself without any available district men as the alarms started coming in on the city desk monitor, he summoned Ennis with the line he always used when about to make an unwelcome assignment: "You may approach the desk and assume the position."

Ennis pushed himself back from his beloved typewriter, a professionally maintained 1947 Royal, and ambled over to the city desk. Harrigan said: "We got a big fire in North Philly that's getting bigger—Northrup Lumber. Get up there and call in something for the B (edition). You're off at midnight, so I'll have someone from the lobster shift (6:30 p.m. to 3:00 a.m.) relieve you."

When he arrived at the lumber yard, it occurred to Ennis that this part of North Philadelphia could pass for South Vietnam. Stacks of framing lumber were sending flames and sparks 30 feet in the air. With the wind as an accomplice, the fire had spread to 17 row homes adjacent to the yard before its advance could be stopped. The heat from the fire had left firemen on the verge of sweating even though the temperatures had tailed off into the 50s. On the periphery of the flames, sparks, smoke, and heat, street shooters from the city's dailies were taking photographs.

Roofs on the row homes were collapsing, sometimes taking expanses of brick wall with them. Policemen were moving briskly down alleyways across the street from the burning houses, trolling for sightseers and looters. Eventually, as the firemen began to control the blaze, the battalion chief took a moment to give Ennis enough that he could call in something at 10:30 for the B.

March 22
When his relief arrived at the fire scene shortly after midnight, Ennis got behind the wheel of his metallic maroon 1968 Chevy Camaro

convertible and started south down Broad Street, headed for a press club called the Quill & Scroll.

Blond and blue-eyed, with a muscular, 5-11 frame that had served him well as a high school running back in Ithaca, N.Y., Ennis would be noticed by the waitresses and barmaids who used the Q&S as an after-hours club. Women found him disconcertingly handsome. Strangers would pinch his ass in bars. A film actress he interviewed took him to bed after allowing that he had Paul Newman eyes and a very sensual mouth. A newsroom intern asked him to drive her home, invited him in, and then blew him before they could finish the bottle of pinot grigio she had purchased for the occasion. His 14-year-old kid sister was implored by girlfriends to call them when he paid a family visit so they could come over and look.

Ennis found a parking space just a block from the Quill & Scroll, which was on a narrow Center City half street. The club had donned its usual Friday night attire: noisy smoke. Editors and reporters from Philadelphia's four dailies, the *Evening Bulletin*, *Philadelphia Inquirer*, *Philadelphia Daily News*, and the *Public Sentinel*, converged on this gritty journalistic salon 50 to 60 strong, anxious to raise their spirits with spirits, to wash away with sterilizing alcohol the newsroom's indigenous tension and imported misery.

The wood paneling in the Quill & Scroll was the color of the bourbon the bartender poured. The once-white ceiling had been tinted an earthy yellow by a decade of cigarette smog. The walls were densely populated with black-framed, pen-and-ink caricatures of local journalistic notables, most of them dead. Through the tar and nicotine haze, Ennis spotted his friend, Bill Guest, at the far end of the bar. He walked over. Guest was enduring a Sean Dunphy monologue on the British abuse of suspected Irish terrorists.

"The Brit bastards keep our lads in their stinking prisons without charging them," Dunphy was saying fervidly. "And they deny them any contact with the outside world. Shades of the SS Argenta, that rotting prison ship moored in Belfast Lough back in 1922. Conditions

12

there were horrible. There was a hunger strike over the detention without trial."

Guest nodded numbly.

Dunphy, a 47-year-old *Public Sentinel* sports writer and the son of immigrants from Belfast, was more Irish than the mayor of Dublin. He loved to lecture Quill & Scroll denizens on the Protestant outrages visited on Northern Ireland's Catholics. Given his bellicose nature after four or five double shots of Irish whiskey, and his past as an amateur light heavyweight boxer, people tended not to suggest to him that IRA hitmen should be prosecuted. More often than not, they elected to suggest nothing at all lest they inadvertently offend him.

Ennis, however, knew Dunphy well enough to know he could tease him a bit if he weren't too fucked up.

He placed his hand on Dunphy's shoulder. "Sean, my dear Borstal boy, I came over here hoping you would regale us with an old favorite or two. How 'bout a chorus of 'Danny Boy' or 'The Rifles of the I.R.A'? You could also lend your mellow Irish tenor to 'The Boys of the Old Brigade.'"

Dunphy grinned. "Ennis, you constipated Brit twit. You lack the cultural grounding to appreciate such ethnic airs."

"Sean, what do you mean? I'm one-eighth Irish. My great-grandmother Doyle came over from Ireland, and only used the word Protestant as an obscenity."

Dunphy smiled and got up to leave, saying he had a date to play spin-the-bottle with someone whose husband was out of town. Ennis took his stool, next to Guest, and ordered a double shot of Windsor Canadian and a Schmidt's draft.

Guest, 61, was a graduate of The Green Eye Shade Era, that romantic interlude that persisted into the post-war years when newspapermen wore felt hats and boozy, itinerant reporters roamed the land, working at a paper for six months or so, sometimes sleeping on a couch in the editor's office, and then moving on.

Guest wasn't one of those gypsies. He was, in fact, a crack

investigative reporter for the Los Angeles Advocate—until he was arrested in a public lavatory for propositioning a handsome young man who turned out to be a handsome young vice cop.

Fired and unable to get work, Guest was found by Philadelphia policemen six months later, passed out in a Center City alley, filthy, reeking of urine, and homeless. The *Public Sentinel*'s editor, Martin Grimsley, who had worked with Guest in Los Angeles, gave him a job as a clerk in the sports department, convinced that if he didn't the man was going to die.

Given their ages and orientations, Guest and Ennis struck some as an odd couple. Rumor quickly had it that the profoundly heterosexual Ennis was, in fact, a switch hitter. But the two men enjoyed their friendship and benefited from its symbiotic nature: Ennis learned from the old newspaper pro, and his cynical mentor found the young man's vitality and enthusiasm pleasantly buoying.

"Man, I'm still coming down from tonight's festivities," Ennis was saying. "It really gets you up: the flames, the crashing roofs, the collapsing walls, firemen yelling. You come down later, thinking of those adults and kids suddenly huddled and homeless. A big fire, it can be so exciting—and so tragic."

"And so disgusting," Guest added. "When I was out on the Coast, a gas explosion set a row of homes on fire. The next morning, I was there when a front-end loader was clearing debris from the basement of one of the gutted houses, and it scooped up the torso of a 14-year-old boy. It wasn't charred. It looked like a nicely done pork roast. It quivered when it was dropped on the ground. It seemed almost gelatinous."

That image took Ennis back to a nascent moment in his career. "I remember the first fatal I ever went out on. A coal truck nailed a little Chevy Corvair and killed the car's four passengers. It was a couple and their two small children. I can still see the coloring books on the floor of the back seat and the red shards of taillight lens scattered on the road like pirate treasure. But most of all, I remember the dead mother being carried to the ambulance on a stretcher. She just jiggled all over, like there wasn't a bone in her body."

Guest nodded knowingly and got up. "Anyway, I'm heading home. I'm halfway through *Rabbit, Run*. Don't know why I'm just getting around to it, it's a great read. You should try it."

"I have," Ennis said of the John Updike novel. "And I loved it."

Ennis looked around the room. Not too many of the female club members had gotten off from work yet, so there was a paucity of potential bedtime stories. But wait. There, at the other end of the bar, was Penelope Rehnquist talking to another barmaid from The Bully Pulpit Bar and Grille.

Over the past two months, Ennis had slept with her four times. She was 25 with delicate features, flawless skin, and enough intellect to get straight A's as a part-time student at Temple University. Ennis liked her body, particularly her breasts. They weren't huge, but they had been inoculated against the gravity virus.

Ennis walked up, unseen, behind the two women and summoned the bartender. "Cedric, would you lavish libations on my two protégées here?" When Penelope turned, he took her hand and kissed it.

"Nothing for me, thanks," said Penelope's co-worker, Rhonda Michaels. "I have to be going."

Ennis ordered drinks for Penelope and himself.

"You smell like smoke," Penelope said.

"The fire department and I were toasting marshmallows up in North Philly," Ennis replied.

Penelope smiled and then allowed that she had "to go potty." She rose from her stool, and let her right hand graze Ennis's groin as she passed him.

The friend left and Penelope returned. Ennis was still standing, and Penelope let her hand again brush his crotch as she took her seat. The contact engendered her variation on a line attributed to Mae West: "Tell me, honey, is that the Eiffel Tower in your pocket, or are you just glad to see me?"

Ennis grinned. "Don't make light of your architectural impact," he said. "As you know, an erection is the sincerest form of flattery."

At 2:20 a.m., they left the club and adjourned to Penelope's studio apartment near 10th and Lombard, where she had to deal with the sincerest form of flattery on three occasions.

After the close encounter of the third kind, Penelope laid back and closed her eyes. Light from the street, rationed by the modest opening between the bedroom curtains, struggled to illuminate her fragile features before dying along her throat.

He propped his chin with his left hand and gazed at her. At this precise moment, even in that lazy light, her face evoked the filigree delicacy of a descending snowflake (which you must catch on cool satin lest it dissolve).

Suddenly, without preamble and without opening her eyes, Penelope asked her bedmate if Bill Guest was a homosexual.

"Bill's my best friend. I don't discuss his personal life."

"From that, I guess I can conclude that his vaginal indifference is considerable," she said.

"Conclude anything you like."

Ennis woke at 11:10 a.m., hungry and mildly hung over. Penelope was still asleep. He rubbed her ass until she opened her eyes.

"Want to get something to eat?"

"No," she said and closed her eyes.

Upon stepping outside Penelope's apartment, beyond her thrall, Ennis felt a sense of loss fencing with a stronger feeling of liberation. He got in his Camaro and gave throaty life to its 283-cubic-inch V-8. He punched the gas pedal and then laid off, just to revel in the engine's burbling baritone subsidence. He loved that engine's note. Nothing like the ballsy throb of a modestly muffled V-8.

The radio came alive with "Different Drum," a two-year-old song performed by Linda Ronstadt and the Stone Poneys: "Yes, I ain't saying you ain't pretty/All I'm saying is I'm not ready/for any person, place or thing/to try and pull the reins in on me . . ."

Ennis drove to his one-bedroom on Washington Square, where he shaved, showered, ate two fried egg sandwiches and a bowl of Wheaties, and then relaxed by the front window before heading to the news room for his ever-changing rewrite shift, this one from 3:00 to 11:00 p.m.

Staring out at the freshly-leafed trees in the square, he marveled, once again, at what seemed like such an improbable journey. He had grown up on a farm near Ithaca, New York. His first newspaper job was in Troy, an even smaller upstate New York community that had the at once pretentious and banal slogan of "Ilium fuit, Troja est" which translates as "Ilium (ancient Troy) was, Troy is."

And now, here he was, working for a major daily in one of America's largest cities, where the vocational voyage had become an adventure.

Penelope awoke an hour after Ennis left. The rumpled void where he had lain evoked the same sense of loss it had generated before, a sense of loss undiluted by one of liberation.

Later that day, Penelope and Rhonda Michaels, her fellow barmaid at The Bully Pulpit, were getting ready for the after-work onslaught of thirsty stockbrokers and store managers.

"I assume you took Ennis home last night," Rhonda said.

"I did."

"What's he like, beyond being drop-dead gorgeous?"

"Well, as you may have noticed, he's got a body to go with that face. He's laid back, a little shy, actually, and not as sophisticated as you would expect someone with his writing facility to be. But, he makes me laugh. And he has this child-like insouciance about him that makes him almost irresistible."

"Sounds like you've got this one under your skin."

"I can't let myself fall for the Prince of Promiscuity."

"I get the feeling you already have."

EDGARTOWN, MA
March 25
Sen. Edward M. Kennedy pled guilty to leaving the scene of a fatal accident in which Mary Jo Kopechne was drowned after he drove a car off the Chappaquiddick Bridge. He received a two-month suspended sentence.

WASHINGTON, D.C.
March 30
The body of General and President Dwight D. Eisenhower was brought by caisson to the Capitol Rotunda to lie in state.

VARIOUS U.S. LOCALES
April 1 to 5
April may not have been the cruelest month in 1969, but in America it generated its share of larceny, arson, riot, death, and injury. It began, innocuously enough, with the resumption of a sit-in at Queens College in Flushing, N.Y. This was followed by the firebombing of the president's home at historically black Alcorn A&M College in Alcorn, Mississippi.

Those first five days also saw the National Guard called into Chicago on the third when black youths went on a rampage on the eve of the first anniversary of the assassination of a non-violent man—the Rev. Dr. Martin Luther King, Jr. They tossed rocks at cars and buses, smashed store windows, and looted. Nearly 300 people were arrested, 72 were injured.

The next morning, on the anniversary of the activist/clergyman's murder, Ennis picked up the book he had been reading—Dr. King's 1967 work, *Where Do We Go From Here: Chaos or Community?*—and thumbed to a passage he wished he had written:

"The ultimate weakness of violence is that it is a descending spiral, begetting the very thing it seeks to destroy. Instead of diminishing evil, it multiplies it. Through violence, you may murder the liar, but you cannot murder the lie, nor establish the truth. Through violence you may murder the hater, but you do not murder hate. So it goes. Returning violence for violence multiplies violence, adding deeper darkness to a night already devoid of stars. Darkness cannot drive out darkness; only light can do that. Hate cannot drive out hate; only love can do that."

Later that day, in Memphis, 8,000 marked the anniversary by marching past the Lorraine Motel where Dr. King was killed. Ennis listened to the KYW account of the march on his car radio, then turned to a pop music station which presently played Dion's recording of "Abraham, Martin and John."

"Anybody here seen my old friend, Martin?/Can you tell me where he's gone?/He freed a lot of people/But it seems the good they die young./I just looked around and he's gone."

On April 5, the day after the anniversary, Donald Lambright, the son of screen comedian Stepin Fetchit, went on a 24-mile shooting spree along the Pennsylvania Turnpike. He fired at 10 or more passing vehicles, killing two and injuring 17 before turning his gun on his wife and himself.

The *Public Sentinel* had four reporters and three photographers spread out along that attenuated concrete killing field, which ended near Harrisburg where police found Lambright and his wife lying dead on the ground by their Pontiac LeMans. The notes recounting the scenes and the interviews with police and survivors flowed into Ennis and fellow rewriteman Saul Lansky. Lansky was handling the news story, Ennis a human interest sidebar derived from survivors' tales of pain, terror and loss.

The murderous spree had begun about 10:00 a.m., and now the 4:25 p.m. copy deadline was looming for the A, the early edition devoted to street sales.

Ennis and Lansky were chain-smoking, creating gardens of crushed butts on the tile floor beneath their feet. The deadline was now 12 minutes away. At this point, as soon as Ennis and Lansky finished a page, or "take," an editor would "railroad" it (give it a cursory edit) and then send it down the tube to the composing room.

The last take of Ennis's sidebar arrived on the city desk four minutes before the copy deadline. Two-and-a-half minutes later, it was in the hands of the composing room foreman, who cut it up into nine one-paragraph slivers and handed a sliver to nine linotype operators, whose machines quickly converted molten lead into nine paragraphs of type. The foreman then assembled those paragraphs in their proper order and dropped them into the waiting page of type on a large, steel table top called "the stone." The page was then handed off to the stereotypers, who converted it into a curved metal plate that was fitted onto a printing press cylinder poised to accelerate out of its starting blocks.

By 6:30, two hours and five minutes after the copy deadline, the *Public Sentinel* was on the streets and Philadelphians were reading about a mentally disturbed 31-year-old's 30-caliber atrocities.

Armed with more reporting from the field, Ennis and Lansky revised and expanded their pieces for the B edition, which would be delivered to homes the next morning. At the end of what turned out to be a 10-hour workday, they adjourned to the Quill & Scroll.

"I have a headache," Ennis observed, pressing a cold glass of vodka and tonic against his forehead. "This job can be a fuckin' pressure cooker."

"Well," Lansky replied, "the *Public Sentinel* never promised we could recline in a summer meadow and write poetry while Elizabeth Taylor peeled us a grape."

Sandwiched between the mayhem and murder during those five days in April were a couple of events that seemed lighthearted by comparison. In Philadelphia, the local Explorer Club chapter's annual dinner featured cocktail hour appetizers made from bone marrow taken from a 50,000-year-old horse found in an Alaskan glacier.

There was also clear evidence, in the April 3 *Public Sentinel*, that kids can do the damnedest things.

"See the wire service piece out of Palm Springs?" Ennis asked Harrigan. When the editor said he hadn't yet, Ennis started reading the wire story: "'An army of 20,000 foraging students and hippies overran this exclusive resort, camping on lawns and stealing food and gas.'

"They brought in 250 cops from a hundred miles around," Ennis added.

"Denny, this is good stuff," he concluded. "Why don't you send me out there?"

"George, if I send you out there, you'll get a sexually transmitted disease from one of those hippie-dippie darlings, and your mother will never forgive me."

"Denny, that's so lame."

"Okay, I'm not going to let you go out there and run up a fat expense account to immortalize a swarm of delinquent locusts. We'll just use wire. Now, go back to your desk and finish that obit I gave you half an hour ago."

GROSSE POINTE FARMS, MI
May 9

Mako was in the woods that bordered the three-acre site of Kenneth Briggs' expansive, half-timbered home in this posh Detroit suburb. He was sitting against an oak tree, with his 35-power binoculars trained on the ersatz Tudor home's one light source: the bedroom that the freshly coronated chairman and president of United Motors shared with his wife, Marsha.

This was the third evening Mako had spent spying on the couple. He now knew that they had martinis at 7:00, sat down to dinner at 8:00, then went into the den to listen to LPs and sip a white wine nightcap. Finally, they would go to their bedroom, read for a while, then put out the lights at about 10:30.

Mako had also learned, by going through their trash, that they had two children away at college and drank varietal wines that he deemed repulsive plonk. Sneaking up to the windows of the illuminated living room and kitchen on the second night of reconnaissance, he noticed deadbolts on the doors—but no evidence of a security system control panel. Since the Briggs had just moved in two weeks before, he reasoned that they simply hadn't gotten around to having a system installed.

Armed with that information, he had formulated the plan he would execute this evening. He waited for an hour after the bedroom lights went out at 10:35, then headed for the house.

After cutting the telephone line, he made his way to the large window over the kitchen sink. The panes in this mullioned window had been installed with putty and glazier's points. He had noticed the night before that the putty was now dried out and cracking loose.

With the help of a penlight, a penknife and a pair of pliers, he quickly scraped away the deteriorated putty around the pane nearest to the window lock, then pulled out the glazier's points securing the pane. He attached a saliva-moistened suction cup to the pane, pulled it out, then reached in and unlocked the window.

Once inside the kitchen, he made a quick equipment check: the shoulder-holstered .45-caliber automatic his uncle had brought home from World War II; the silencer for the .45 in his right front pants pocket; the backup 22-caliber revolver holstered on his right ankle, a sheathed Bowie knife on his belt, and the canvas duffle bag he would use to carry away the valuables after he made the hits. All present and accounted for.

He pulled off his loafers, flicked on his flashlight, affixed the silencer to the .45, and padded through the kitchen, dining room, and then the living room, where stairs led to the second-floor bedrooms. He turned right at the top of the stairs and headed for the master bedroom. The Briggs had left the hall light on, which meant they wouldn't see light from a flashlight leaking under the door.

Mako knew from his surveillance (which included a tree climb) that there was a light switch just to the left of the doorway and that the couple's queen-size bed would be situated about six feet beyond. He drew the .45 automatic. The first round was already chambered, so all he had to do was release the safety. He flung open the door, flicked on the light, and fired.

The bullets that initially struck Briggs were from a weapon the Army formally referred to as an automatic pistol. But the 1911 model .45 is actually a semi-automatic, meaning that it fires only once each time you pull the trigger. The bullet it launches is almost a half-inch in diameter. Given its weight, this slug has a rather leisurely muzzle velocity of 850 feet per second. But that hefty mass imparts considerable shocking power at close range.

Briggs was lying on his left side with his right arm across his wife's abdomen when the first bullet hit him in the back and drove him into her side. Already wounded when that initial round passed through her husband and into her, she took a second bullet to the chest and a third to the forehead. The fourth bullet entered the forehead of her already-dead husband.

Mako was wearing latex gloves to prevent fingerprints and had worn them when he loaded the .45's magazine. Still, he picked up the spent brass just to be safe.

He then retrieved the duffle he had left in the kitchen and started filling it with such stuff as burglaries are made of.

Mrs. Briggs had some valuable jewelry. There was also antique English flatware in the dining room, two Picasso pen-and-inks in the living room, and a rather forgettable but still valuable Rothko print in the foyer.

Mako gathered up his decoy plunder and drove off in a rented '69 Ford Fairlane sedan.

A few minutes before midnight, he threw his rock-weighted bag of booty into the Detroit River, near where it begins at Lake St. Clair. Dumping the Picasso and Rothko pieces bothered him. Their destruction struck him as criminal.

PHILADELPHIA, PA

May 10

Three hours into his four p.m. to midnight rewrite shift Ennis returned from the newsroom lavatory just in time for the discovery of the Mystery Shitter's latest deposit.

No one knew how the legendary Mystery Shitter could drop a pile of excrement by the desk of night city editor Harrigan, in the midst of a heavily populated news room, and not be noticed. But he had been doing it, about once a month, for the last six months. It was theorized that he transported the turds in a poop-proof bag secreted inside his sport coat, and then dumped the bag's contents when no one was looking.

"Goddammit," Harrigan yelled, kicking his chair into the aisle next to the city desk. "I'm going to catch that bastard. Then I'm going to rip off his dick and shove it up his ass."

"Denny, it's not like you to get so emotional, so unprofessional," Ennis said.

Harrigan glared at him. "And that, my smart-ass pretty boy, is going to cost you. It may not be tonight, it might be three nights from now. But one evening, a truly awful, monumentally disgusting story is going to present itself, and you will be the poor son of a bitch to trot up here and assume the position."

"But Chief, often in the evenings in the Great Wigwam, I have spoken to the braves, the squaws and the children of your kindness and fairness, of your ceaseless hatred for vindictiveness."

"Here," Harrigan said, handing him a clipping from the *Bulletin*. "Rewrite this for the B."

It was an obituary for a 20-year-old corporal from the city's Grays Ferry section who had been killed in Vietnam. The piece was only six paragraphs long and rife with obit boiler plate. Ennis felt that a kid two years removed from the senior prom, who was killed in the service of his country, deserved something more than this formulaic half-effort.

Ennis called the home of the dead soldier's parents. When his father answered, the reporter asked him if he could come to the house and speak with him about his son. When Clarence Reynolds said he could, Ennis told Harrigan he was taking his dinner break and then headed to the Reynolds' modest, brick rowhouse in Grays Ferry.

Reynolds opened the door, limply shook Ennis's hand, and then motioned to a well-used burgundy velour easy chair. Ennis sat down and Reynolds took a seat four feet away on a chocolate brown, leatherette sofa.

"So, what would you like to know, Mr. Ennis?"

"Well, sir, perhaps we could start with you telling me a little about the kind of person your son was."

Reynolds rubbed a finger across his right eyebrow. "He was a gentle boy, Teddy. When he enlisted in the Army—yes, he enlisted, he wasn't drafted—I couldn't, for the life of me, imagine him killing anybody. Hell, I couldn't even get him to go small game hunting."

Reynolds, a maintenance man in a South Philadelphia soft pretzel bakery, leaned back wearily and trained his bloodshot eyes on the ceiling. "You know, he thought he was doing the right thing, the patriotic thing, going over to that godforsaken place. He was acting in good faith, and for these slapped-ass, draft-dodgin' fucks from the suburbs to suggest there was something criminal about what he did over there just makes me crazy. You know, I can understand why they might not want to go over there and get their asses blown off, but they got no right sayin' that."

Reynolds' rage subsided, and a gentler soliloquy went on for another 15 minutes. It was filled with affectionate anecdotes about his son and ended with the swing set he had built for him.

"I made the frame and the seats out of cedar and used stainless steel bolts and chains. The thing will last forever. When Teddy outgrew it, I took it apart and put it out in the lawn shed thinking that, one day, I would bolt it back together for his kids.

"I don't know now," he said, daubing his eyes with a soggy

Kleenex. "There's a single mom down the street with a couple kids swing set age. Maybe I'll see if she wants me to put it up in her backyard."

Ennis borrowed pictures of Teddy in his gray high school graduation gown and his Army uniform and headed back to the office. He went right to his desk and started writing the story of someone who was barely old enough to shave every day when he was torn apart by a land mine. The piece began:

"Clarence Reynolds made the swing set for his son, Teddy, from cedar and stainless steel. He wanted it to last. When Teddy outgrew it, his father disassembled it and stored it in the lawn shed behind his Grays Ferry rowhouse, expecting to reassemble it one day for Teddy's kids.

"That's not going to happen . . ."

Harrigan, a paunchy 45-year-old with five kids and an ungainly mortgage, looked up from the Reynolds piece he had just edited and called Ennis over.

"I thought I was getting a six-inch obit. Instead, I get this 23-inch whore's dream."

He stared sternly at Ennis, eliciting the intended disappointment, and then smiled. "This is a nice, nice piece, George. I wish I'd get more like it. I'm going to lobby the operations desk to put it out front."

"Thanks, Denny," Ennis said, turning to leave.

"Oh, and George, you're no longer a candidate for that bag-of-shit story I promised you."

Ennis walked back to his desk, Harrigan's praise amplifying his writer's high. (That euphoria is a feeling you get when you've written something that really flows, and you just know that it's the best you can do and it's pretty damn good.)

The elation quotient rose even more when Harrigan subsequently told him the piece would, in fact, be going to page one.

May 13

Ennis was working the 10:30 a.m. to 6:30 p.m. shift, so he was in the thrall of Seth Menges, the day city editor. The editor got off the phone and looked Ennis's way.

"George, I'm going to have to ask you to spend the day down at the 'Roundhouse' (police headquarters)."

"Seth, I'm a rewrite man. Are you demoting me?"

"George, our Roundhouse reporter called in sick. We are defenseless against a horde of competitors, so I want you to go down there and emulate the 300 heroic Spartans who battled Xerxes' huge Persian army at Thermopylae."

Ennis smiled. "Okay, since you've elevated me to the rank of hero, I'll be happy to volunteer."

"Actually, George, volunteering was never an option for you."

Down at the Roundhouse, where Ennis had spent a year as a police reporter near the outset of his *Public Sentinel* tenure, he encountered a news day slow enough to evoke the progress of a one-legged centipede. After several hours of nothing rising much above the level of a tree-marooned house cat, he phoned the man in the pork pie hat, Capt. Lawrence J. Weatherford, head of the narcotics squad. When the police beat turned into a Sahara, and the A deadline was looming, the captain was the man to call. Capt. Weatherford loved publicity more than life.

"Captain, this is George Ennis from the *Public Sentinel*. There's absolutely nothing on the blotter. I was hoping you had something that would give us a crime story we could play big."

"Give me an hour, my boy," Capt. Weatherford said.

Fifty-five minutes later, Weatherford called back: "We have just arrested a South Philadelphia drug dealer known as the Maharajah of Marijuana. This is one of the biggest drug busts in city history. We're talking dope with a street value of at least 200 large ($1,657,367 in 2023 dollars)."

The captain gave Ennis the rest of the arrest details and allowed that he would be available for photographs showing him placing the foul felon in a cell. Ennis said he would get a photographer right on it.

"Thanks, captain," Ennis said finally.

"Think nothing of it, my boy."

May 22

Roger Heeney, the paper's recently appointed travel editor, came into the newsroom at 10:00 a.m. to finish his piece on Venice in spring, based on a four-day sojourn. In it, he checked all the Venetian cliché boxes, from the gondola ride to the glassblowing demonstration, in a quite readable fashion.

The travel beat was a nice gig that fit right in with the high school graduate's vocational strategy, which was getting over on the college boys in charge of the news room. Indeed, Heeney would much rather con his way into a cushy sinecure than do the solid news work of which he was quite capable. Prior to becoming the paper's travel editor, his coups had included a virtually work-free, month-long sabbatical in an Australian newsroom and a *Public Sentinel* assignment to report on the troubles in Northern Ireland, which he covered by reading the Irish newspapers in a Belfast pub.

Rumor had it that Heeney got the travel job by serving as the news room stool pigeon for *Public Sentinel* editor Grimsley. Ennis concluded this was more than a rumor when Grimsley brought up the fact that Ennis had had several drinks at Lansky's cousin's house, and then took the cousin's Harley for a spin during which he went off the road and over the handlebars. Ennis confronted him about this shortly after the travel editor arrived in the news room.

"Thanks for telling Grimsley about me dropping the bike after I had some drinks," Ennis said.

"I didn't tell him," Heeney countered." It must have been someone else."

"You're the only person I told."

Heeney fell silent.

"You ever rat me out to management again, Roger, and I'm not just going to spread it around that you're Grimsley's ear. I'm going to fuck you up."

May 24

It was late Saturday afternoon, and Ennis was working the 1:00 to 10:00 p.m. shift for Sam Ferguson, the weekend day city editor.

"George, the Philadelphia news scene so far today is deader than a dinosaur's dick," Ferguson said. "Absolutely nothing is happening. So. I have an idea."

Ennis felt a psychic shiver at the prospect of being presented with an editor's story idea on a slow news day.

"There's a preview party this evening for an important exhibition opening at the art museum. In addition to the Main Line aristocrats, it probably will draw some city movers and shakers. Tate (Mayor James Tate) and Rizzo (Police Commissioner Frank Rizzo) might well make an appearance. So, why don't you go over there and hang out? You might get something—Rizzo's always good copy—and, at the very least, it'll be more fun than sitting around here contemplating your navel. Just check in with me every half hour or so in case something breaks.

"Oh, and you'll also get a chance to see Society Sue in action. Be ready for that. Legend has it that she jumps out from behind potted palms and asks the people she doesn't know: 'What's your name and what do they call you?'"

Society Sue was Susan Dirkson, the leading Philadelphia society writer that the *Public Sentinel*'s publisher, C. Everett Manning, had hired away from the *Bulletin* at no small expense to help him get a foothold in Philadelphia society. But the old-family aristocrats were well aware that Manning's fortune sprang from his father's rum-running during Prohibition, and they were not at all disposed to letting him become one of the gang.

After Manning's quest for old guard acceptance was derailed, Dirkson continued to cover Philadelphia society for the *Public Sentinel*. She was an indefatigable chronicler of the elite, who often would attend two or three social events in a single evening in a never-ending quest for the wit and wisdom of people whose wit and wisdom were often less considerable than their inherited wealth. In addition to her obsession with the elites' silly nicknames—like Biff and Bitsy—she was a master of the uninstructive quote, as Ennis was reminded when he later read her account of the preview party. It included this:

"Andrew D. 'Buffy' Cadwalader 1V, who had been circulating among the guests, stopped to chat with me. He said, 'I just had a gin and tonic. I think I'll have another. Would you like one?'"

In the end, the reception proved more productive for Dirkson than for Ennis. Rizzo and Tate didn't show, and the politicians who did invariably performed the Dance of Ambiguity.

Back in the newsroom, Ennis revealed his failed story crop to Ferguson, who told him to chalk it up to experience—and get him something on a fiery fatal on I-95.

MONTREAL, QUEBEC
May 26
John Lennon and Yoko Ono opened their second Bed-in, this one an eight-day sleepover in the Queen Elizabeth Hotel. In the course of it, Lennon composed and recorded "Give Peace a Chance."

PHILADELPHIA, PA
June 2
Ennis leaned back in his leather Chesterfield and briefed Penelope on the be-in he had covered earlier in the evening on Fairmount Park's Belmont Plateau. "The usual scene, kids doing a little heterosexual handling, and the scent of pot wafting through the forest primeval. I love the narcs trying to catch the potheads. They really blend with their Ban-Lon shirts and black socks with sandals.

30

"Blind Bob was there too, of course."

Penelope looked at him quizzically. "Blind Bob?"

"He's a reporter for the *Philadelphia Insider*, one of those giveaway weeklies. He covers this sort of thing a lot and invariably comes up with a zingy quote to end the story. That grabby kicker is always unattributed, and that's led us suspicious news types to believe he's fabricating blind quotes—hence, Blind Bob."

June 4

Ennis walked into the newsroom at 3:00 p.m., just in time to witness a performance by the mercurial Saul Lansky, the husky co-worker who sat at the desk next to his. Lansky was taking deadline notes from Martha Lindner, who had covered a meeting of the City Planning Commission. She had gotten a job with the paper as a teenager during World War II, when male reporters were in short supply. She lived in terror of error. She avoided errors of omission by starting at the beginning of her notes and regurgitating every word until she reached the end. That way, no one could say she skipped something important.

Frequently, rewrite men would say what Lansky was now saying: "Martha, I have to write a page-and-a-half for the A, and, as you know, that deadline is just a half hour away. So, could you please tell me the important developments at this meeting, the highlights?"

Lindner then did what she always did when asked to sum up: She went back to the beginning of her notes and began reciting them all over again.

Seething with frustration and rage, Lansky jumped to his feet, ripped off his headset, and fired it at the desktop. Pieces of the device scattered. He then climbed on his desk, stood up with fists clenched on high, and yelled: "My mind is turning to oatmeal!"

"That's too Irish," Ennis said, as Lansky descended from his desktop oration. "A Jewish cerebral cortex should turn into kugel."

Lansky smiled and ran his hand back through his thinning hair as if guiding its retreat from his forehead. He was 31, six feet tall, and a burly 225 pounds. He wasn't handsome, but he was a very masculine presence whose outrageous behavior made women laugh. They typically saw him as funny, powerful, yet teddy-bear cuddly. This was a turn-on for some. As a consequence, he sometimes slept with women out of his aesthetic league, like the lovely editor of the society page.

When his shift ended at 11:00, Ennis headed for the Quill & Scroll. He stepped inside and saw Penelope sitting alone at the end of the bar.

"Penelope! Where've you been? I haven't seen you in weeks."

"I've been seeing someone."

"Are you free this evening?"

"No."

"How 'bout tomorrow night?"

"I'm afraid I'm otherwise engaged."

"Otherwise engaged? What the hell is this, a scene from a Noel Coward play?" A pause and then: "I guess I'm a bit surprised. I thought you and I had some good times."

"We did. But I was ready for something more—a relationship and the things that go with it."

"Like what?"

"The things my new friend and I do. We have meals together, we play Scrabble, we have conversations."

"You and I have had conversations."

"George, we never had a stand-alone conversation. Our conversations were always sexual bookends."

"But there was some pretty good body language between those bookends."

"Yes, there was. But women do not live by orgasm alone, at least not this one. Anyway, I have to go."

"What's his name?"

"Jerry."

She picked up her purse and walked out. She was one of many

women in his life, and he didn't think he was in love with her. Still, her departure triggered an ambiguous sense of loss. And this time, it wasn't offset by a feeling of liberation.

June 5

After Penelope left, at 12:05 a.m., Ennis walked up the bar and joined Guest. They had a couple pops and talked sports. Presently, Ennis let his eyes prospect the room for likely ladies. He spotted a *Public Sentinel* colleague, Janet Goddard, sitting alone at the end of the bar. By the 60s, newspaperwomen were ending their traditional incarcerations on the women's pages in significant numbers and finding seats in a men's club called The Newsroom.

Janet Goddard was a good reporter and a better writer than most of her male co-workers. She was also a comely woman of 29 with a body that never abandoned its quest for perfection. Ennis thought her breasts, generously sized and perfectly sculpted, were among the Seven Wonders of the Sexual World. They were known around the newsroom as Janet's Planets.

She also really liked sex. The first time Ennis slept with her, she tore a button off his shirt in her haste to remove it. And she was one of the few women he ever got off by simply pinching a nipple.

The only thing she liked better than sex was risky sex. That really excited her. When they sneaked down to her roomy sedan in the *Public Sentinel* parking lot one evening, he had to clamp his hand over her mouth at each orgasmic juncture.

Ennis finished admiring her accoutrements and turned to Guest.

"Well, Bill, I think it's time to cut one out of the herd."

Guest smiled wearily and pulled at the outside corners of his eyes with the thumb and middle finger of his left hand. "George, there is a condition known as sex addiction. I understand it can be treated. Maybe you should seek the help of a therapist before your dick falls off."

"Dr. Guest, if I have this affliction, and I sure as hell hope I do, I will not seek medical help. Of course, if I learn that it leads to blindness, like masturbation, I'll just sleep around 'til I need glasses.

"Seriously, Bill, my assorted couplings are not merely libidinous. They are also acts of altruism. They are a kind of psycho-physical therapy in which I utilize various stimuli to relieve the sexual tensions of women."

Guest rose from his bar stool. "I'm going to leave now, George, before the solid waste gets high enough to cause a knee infection."

Guest headed for the door and Ennis headed for Janet. He drew next to her and put his arm around her.

"Janet, I was gazing at you from afar and becoming so overwrought. I believe you have turned all the ligaments in my knees into overcooked linguine."

She looked up at him through glazed eyes. She was working on her third martini. But she was still aware enough to know that his and her positions at the end of the bar were such that no one could see her reach over with her left hand and squeeze his balls.

"You say hello in a universal language, a kind of Braille Esperanto," Ennis said.

Outside, they climbed in the Camaro, and Ennis turned the ignition key. The engine came to life and so did the radio. Kenny Rogers and The First Edition musicians were part way through a rather acidic song: "I pushed my soul in a deep dark hole and then I followed it in/I watched myself crawlin' out as I was a-crawlin' in/I got up so tight I couldn't unwind/I saw so much I broke my mind/I just dropped in to see what condition my condition was in . . ."

Janet leaned over, unzipped his fly, and slipped her hand inside.

"I just dropped in to see what condition your condition was in," she said.

June 6

Guest was checking the expense accounts of the sports columnists and beat writers before passing them on to Finance when he came across the one handed in by a sports columnist named Horst Dietrich. The man was arrogant, overbearing, and only mildly talented. But he knew enough about the sex life of Martin Grimsley, the *Public Sentinel*'s editor, to get and retain his column.

Guest walked across the sports department to where Dietrich was sitting and showed him an expense account entry for $11 ($92 in 2023 currency) that was attributed to "drinks with a source" and submitted without a receipt.

"Do you think we should elaborate on this? Guest asked.

"No," the columnist replied, absently rubbing a neck scar that veered very close to his right carotid artery.

Dietrich was disdainful of the small, frail man who had fallen from journalistic grace and treated him like an indentured servant. Guest responded by wearing his hatred on his frayed sleeve.

Dietrich's expenses also included those incurred on a trip to Detroit. That sojourn rang a bell for Guest, but he didn't know where the sound was coming from.

Later in the afternoon, Harrigan abruptly ended his phone conversation with Larry Arabis, a bearded rewrite man who talked a lot about weed and acid and had a large peace symbol emblazoned on the back of his Army surplus combat jacket (which he would replace with a sport coat if he had to go out on assignment). The night city editor raised his eyes heavenward, and then looked out over the newsroom.

"Lawrence of Arabis will not be joining us this evening," he announced to no one in particular. "When I asked him if he was ill he said, 'No, I just can't get it together, and that leaves me too distracted to work.'"

Harrigan seethed a bit, then got up and strode back to the company nurse's office, where he had his blood pressure taken. He was obsessed with his blood pressure and readily defended its Everest elevation when unmedicated against less credentialed challengers. When a colleague would mention his hypertension, Harrigan would ask what his pressure was sans medication and then say things like, "Huh, you think that's high? You should see mine. I mean, hell, 170 over 95, that's child's play."

June 7

Twenty hours after the announcement of his inability to get it together, Arabis ambled in for the lobster shift, resplendent in backpack and scruffy beard.

"Well, Sir Lawrence, were you able to get it together?" Harrigan asked.

"No, but I thought I better bring it all in here, anyway."

"That's good thinking," Harrigan said, "because your un-together self was about to become your unemployed self."

Shortly after Lawrence of Arabis's 6:30 p.m. return to the newsroom, Guest took his dinner break. But instead of going to the cafeteria, he rode the elevator up to the *Public Sentinel*'s library. Dietrich's Detroit trip had been bothering him. The veteran investigative reporter had this feeling that it was related to something, but he couldn't grow the connective tissue. So he went to the library's back issue rack and began looking at *Public Sentinels* for the dates when the columnist was in Detroit. If this didn't yield anything, he planned to consult *The Detroit Free Press*.

But the front page of the May 11 *Public Sentinel* divulged the connection: The new chairman of United Motors and his wife had been found shot to death the day before in their suburban Detroit home.

June 8

Guest was back in the *Public Sentinel*'s library at 8:00 on this Sunday morning. He knew that Dietrich being in Detroit on the day of the murders was almost certainly a coincidence. And yet, there was an infinitesimal possibility that it wasn't, and that's what brought him in here on his day off.

Guest had begun his research two days before by obtaining copies of Dietrich's expenses for the past three years. From those expense accounts, he made a list of where Dietrich had been and when. Now, he was in the library, perusing the *Public Sentinel* editions on microfilm that corresponded to the dates of Dietrich's travels.

The results were compelling. In nearly a third of the cases, Dietrich's trips coincided with a high-profile murder. This included some instances in which he would take a couple vacation days to extend his stay before flying home on the company nickel. Guest also noticed that whenever the lethal bullet was mentioned in the news stories, it was always .45 caliber.

This was exciting, and not just because Guest despised Dietrich. Like his vocational kin, the old reporter loved it when he pulled the research lever and the investigative slot machine rewarded him with three cherries. And this, he felt, could also be a substantial jackpot.

Guest was almost 62 and a man with modest pension prospects. He had thought of living on the beach somewhere, in Mexico, the Caribbean, or Florida. It occurred to him that Dietrich's moonlighting had engendered some serious bucks and that a one-time demand on those funds would buy him an oceanfront place to live, a place where his Social Security and small pensions from the *Guardian* and the *Public Sentinel* would give him enough to get along.

Guest considered writing a blackmail note to Dietrich based on what he had learned but decided against it. He reasoned that what he had, finally, was not really actionable. There was no hard proof here. The coinciding dates could be explained away as coincidence. And while Dietrich's expensive house and Italian sports car might suggest spending beyond his means, an inheritance rumored to be substantial and the fact that his housemate sister was employed would get him off that hook.

So, Guest's commute to retirement found itself in an evidentiary traffic snarl. He decided some reconnaissance was in order.

June 9

Janet Goddard stepped inside her one-bedroom apartment and walked immediately to the refrigerator. She removed a bottle of 100-proof Stolichnaya vodka from the freezer and poured about six ounces into a tumbler. Armed with the vodka and another glass filled with orange juice, she kicked off her shoes, sat back on a white leather sofa, and started chasing down generous gulps of Stoli with the fruit juice.

She drained the glass of vodka in six minutes and then rolled a joint. The vodka was already starting to kick in by the time she took the first toke. This was Janet's after-work ritual: a big drink on an empty stomach, followed by a joint. Increasingly, she had been adding LSD to the menu, although she didn't drop acid this time.

Ten minutes later, feeling pleasantly buzzy, she telephoned Ennis, who lived four blocks from her Center City high-rise.

"George, whatcha up to?"

"Nothin' much. Just working on a short story *The New Yorker* probably won't want."

"Come on over, then."

"What did you have in mind?" Ennis asked, with mild theatricality.

She chuckled. "I was hoping we could do unspeakable things to each other, acts only hinted at in *The Deviant's Guide to Egregious Kinkyosity*."

"What a relief! I thought for a moment you wanted to make an innocent farm boy do something unorthodox."

"I was thinking of novel destinations for bodily fluids," she replied.

"But I was in such a puritanical mood," Ennis said. "I wanted to make pilgrim love to you through a hole in your bed sheet. And that's the safe thing to do, you know. Looking at that Sodom and Gomorrah body of yours, uncensored by bed sheets, might just cause me to turn into a pillar of salt."

"Actually, only a part of you would turn into a pillar—a rather small part in your case."

"My dear woman, penis insult is no more attractive than penis envy."

"George, I was just pulling your chain. Your propagative parts are quite adequate."

"Say," Ennis said then, "if I do come over, do you promise not to tie me up and hurt me?"

"George, could it be that you're distrustful of women? Could it be that you really don't like ladies very much, that beneath that aw-shucks, flannel-shirted, agrarian veneer dwells a raving misogynist?"

"A misogynist, moi?" Ennis said. "Why, some of my best friends are of the feminine persuasion. By the way, you sound a little buzzy."

"I may have ventured a toke or two over the line."

"I'll be over in about ten minutes."

The evening started on a rather mundane note: fellatio and the missionary position. Janet then suggested a shower. As she finished soaping his back and shoulders, she moved around to his right side and clamped his thigh with her legs, rubbing her labia against it. She then began pissing on his outer thigh. As her bladder emptied, Ennis heard a low moan and felt her pussy shudder. A mild orgasm?

"That certainly was a novel destination for bodily fluids," Ennis conceded.

After they had rinsed off, Janet started rigorously toweling her hair, inspiring her truly inspiring breasts to perform erotic calisthenics on her rib cage. Ennis hardened again. He dropped to his knees in front of her, nuzzled her damp pubic hair, then trained his blue kryptonite eyes on hers. "If you are done urinating on me, perhaps I could initiate my vaginal investigation," he said.

Janet smiled, ran her fingers through his blond mane, and said: "Cunnilingus as scientific inquiry. An interesting concept."

After he got her off, she gently grasped his erection like a rudder and steered him back into the bedroom.

Later, on Janet's four-poster, a satiated Ennis surveyed her Mt. Rushmore mammaries.

"Some breasts barely merit a lecture mention," he said, "but yours are a legitimate three-credit course. They're not just glorious. They're apocalyptic. Surely, this is the chest that launched a thousand stiffies."

"Thank you, kind mammophile," Janet said. "Is this where I say something poetic about your pulsing pylon of passion?"

June 11

Guest was huddled near a large forsythia in the backyard of Horst Dietrich's stone colonial in Bryn Mawr, a town in an affluent Philadelphia suburban area called the Main Line. On day shift this week, Guest had been able to devote the last three evenings to this surveillance.

Dietrich, 31, a lanky 6-5 with sharp features, long slender fingers, and short, receding brown hair, lived here with his unmarried sister, Gretchen, 28. Guest noticed on the previous two nights that when they went upstairs to bed, the lights went on in only one bedroom.

On this, the third night, he watched through a dining room window as Dietrich followed his sister into the kitchen. He crept up to the kitchen's back window and looked in through the three-inch gap between the curtains. The scene on the island counter was something out of *The Postman Always Rings Twice*, except Dietrich had initially substituted cunnilingus for intercourse. The window was open on this still, warm June night, but Gretchen's gasps and moans and the couple's concentration minimized the chance they would see or hear the man crouched outside the window, snapping pictures with his expensive Minolta. He got seven shots with Dietrich's head between her thighs, then three more after he stood up and penetrated her.

Guest slipped back to the safety of the forsythia, then headed through a stand of trees to the street where he had parked his '63 Ford Falcon. He started the car and turned on the radio. Presently, the title song from the musical, *Hair*, came on: "Gimme a head with hair/Long, beautiful hair/Shining, gleaming/Streaming, flaxen, waxen/Gimme down to there hair/Shoulder length or longer hair/Here baby, there mama/Everywhere daddy, daddy . . ."

He thought of Gretchen's long chestnut mane and its rapturous swirling. He thought, too, about the retirement that would be generated by the fruits of his darkroom.

Meanwhile, Gretchen Dietrich was sitting at the dresser in the bedroom she shared with her brother (she had a studio apartment in Center City but rarely used it) combing her hair and thinking about her life. Primarily, she thought about her older brother. She had been sleeping with him for half her life, since she was 14 and he was 17. It started one night on the sofa while their parents were out, and continued almost every day after school.

She had liked the sex but worried about the incest. Her older brother told her that incest was a social taboo designed to prevent inbreeding and that as long as he used a prophylactic, that wouldn't be a problem. (He used condoms until age 21, when, in the interests of enhanced safety and pleasure, he had a vasectomy.)

She cared for her dominant brother and hadn't thought about being unfaithful to him until recently, when she discovered lipstick on a shirt collar and a pair of underpants while doing his laundry.

She was hurt and angry. She had devoted the last 14 years of her life to a monogamous relationship apparently as fictional as it was aberrant. But she wasn't about to confront her brother. The Horst-induced orgasms were matched by Horst-induced fear. He had a vile temper and she didn't know what he might do.

Still, she thought about a new life, a life that included sex with unrelated men.

READING, PA
June 12
Ennis had taken this Friday off and driven 60 miles to the center of Reading to watch the filming of *Rabbit, Run*. He loved the John Updike novel, partly because he felt such a strong kinship with the title character, a former high school athlete like himself.

While the scene to be filmed was readied, a PR man handed Ennis a press release. Among other things, it said that Updike had declined an offer to write the script for this film version of his book, saying the characters had left him. (Little ever left John Updike, of course, and certainly not the main characters, who went on to populate several *Rabbit, Run* sequels.)

A young actor named James Caan was playing Rabbit, and he chatted with Ennis about the character.

"He's a very physical guy," Caan said of Rabbit. "You know the scene where he's running down the alley after he's decided to quit smoking? He doesn't just drop the pack in a trash can, he fires it up in the air."

Caan went on about Harry "Rabbit" Angstrom. His take on the character struck Ennis as quite perceptive.

The scene being filmed, a brief one, had Rabbit sleeping in his car, waiting for Coach Tothero to show up at the gym. When his old high school coach arrives, Rabbit jumps out of the car, calls out his name, and goes over to greet him.

Director Jack Smight was sitting in a high, canvas chair at the scene's edge when Ennis walked up and introduced himself.

"I'm a big fan of the book," he told Smight.

"Well, the script follows the book very closely," Smight observed.

Ennis smiled. "Well, to follow the book you should have had him getting out of a '55 Ford, not this clapped-out Caddy convertible."

Smight started to respond, then settled on not being amused.

PHILADELPHIA, PA

June 13

Guest wrote an unsigned note to Dietrich and mailed it, along with prints of the surveillance shots, to his home. The note read:

"I know that in at least 12 cases over the past three years you have been in a city when a notable person was assassinated. I also know that a .45 caliber bullet was often recovered in the victims or at the crime scene. I suspect ballistics would show that the same gun—could it be your gun?—was used in every case.

"But, I'm sure you are coming to the same conclusion that I did: that I don't have enough to put you in jail. However, if you look at the photographs in the enclosed envelope, you will see that I do have enough to at least make you leave the *Public Sentinel* in disgrace.

"What I'm proposing is a one-time payment of $25,000 ($209,665 in 2023 dollars). That would give you the negatives and end it all. I wouldn't come after you again.

"There's a trash can on the southeast corner of Fitler Square. I want you to place a sack containing the $30,000 in $100 bills in that trash can at 9:30 p.m. on the evening of Friday, June 20. As soon as I see that you have done so and left the square, I will pick up the money and drop the negatives in the mail.

"And don't even think about hanging around after the drop to kill me. I have retained prints of the 10 photographs, which I've placed in a safety deposit box, along with my research on your hits. I have given a key to that box to a friend, with instructions to open it in the event of my death or disappearance."

June 15
Dietrich opened the envelope in the study of his tastefully furnished stone home. There was a note and another envelope inside. He read the note, then opened the envelope that accompanied it. It took a lot to rattle Dietrich, but those photographs succeeded.

He willed himself to put aside the fear and rage and try to figure out who was attempting to blackmail him. Obviously, he reasoned, it was someone who knew when he traveled and then matched those time frames to the corresponding hits. Someone like that hateful little sports department clerk.

The pictures were land mines that represented a huge loose end. Dietrich hated loose ends. He hated them as much as the man he now believed to be the blackmailer.

"That pathetic little faggot," Dietrich said to an empty living room.

"Does he really think he can do this to me, Horst Dietrich?"

Gretchen appeared in the doorway. "Horst, I heard you say something. You seemed upset. Are you okay?"

"Fine, dear. Go on up now. I'll join you in a moment."

Dietrich slumped back in his Le Corbusier chair and savored the last sip from a glass of Chambertin '47. He had found two bottles of this wine in a victim's cellar. And they weren't filled with a merely superb, "run-of-the-mill" Chambertin '47. These two bottles contained Chambertin aristocracy: Antonin Rodet Chambertin Grand Cru, Côte de Nuits.

He sniffed the empty glass, seeking a parting evocation of greatness, and made a decision: He would show up at Fitler Square and place a $30,000 package in the trash can. Doing this would serve several purposes, he reasoned. First, compliance would prevent an immediate, devastating response by the blackmailer. Secondly, from a hiding place near Fitler Square, he could determine if Guest was indeed the blackmailer. If it didn't turn out to be Guest, the surveillance would probably reveal who the shakedown artist was. He could then plan how to end the problem and get his money back.

June 16

Boris Levandowski arrived in the newsroom before the start of his 4:00 to midnight shift armed with assorted tools, a hasp, and a muscular brass padlock. He set to work installing the hasp on the bottom drawer of his linoleum-topped gray steel desk.

Levandowski had established himself as the newsroom wifty largely by obsessing over the contents of his desk. Like the Bogart character in *The Treasure of the Sierra Madre*, who was given to accusing his fellow miners of messing with his "goods," Levandowski was forever charging that someone had gone into his desk drawers and taken some of his possessions.

"Items are missing," he would report with incensed ambiguity.

But he had the solution. After installing the hasp, he put his goods in the bottom drawer and locked it with the big padlock.

The security work completed, Levandowski rose, placed his hands on his hips, and smiled at his handiwork. Then he turned toward the city desk and smirked. Shortly afterward, Harrigan gave Levandowski a reporting assignment in South Philadelphia, partly because he wasn't much of a rewrite man, and partly because he was such a pain in the ass.

After Levandowski left the newsroom, Lansky jumped up on his desk and made an announcement: "A deed of Homeric proportion has come to me in a dream."

Whereupon, he walked over to Levandowski's desk and removed the top drawer. He then reached down into the opening, lifted out the contents of the padlocked bottom drawer, replaced the top drawer, and secreted the goods in an unused desk on the other side of the newsroom.

Levandowski returned two hours later and went berserk when he discovered the theft of his goods. Harrigan calmed him down by promising "an immediate hard-target search of every desk drawer, closet, and umbrella stand in the newsroom."

"Ennis and Lansky, give us a hand," Harrigan said with considerable gravity. "We won't rest until the stolen property is recovered."

After five minutes of the search charade, Harrigan uncovered the purloined goods.

"Over here," Harrigan said, "I think we found it."

Boris rushed over and peered in the cardboard carton containing his goods.

"Is it all there, Boris?"

"I think so."

"Well," Harrigan concluded gravely, "if that's the case, I don't see any point in embarrassing the paper by alerting the authorities to what was obviously a prank. Don't you agree, Boris?"

Levandowski nodded grudgingly.

After Levandowski walked off to the men's room, a smiling Harrigan instructed his colleagues on the desk not to bother him with mundane matters like editing stories.

"I must work on my Levandowski biography," he explained. "It's entitled, *One Flew Over the Cuckoo's Desk*."

Two hours later, at 11:55 p.m., the night city editor's face suddenly reddened with rage. A lingual sluice gate opened, and a mighty flood of obscenities gushed forth. The Mystery Shitter had struck again, and Harrigan had stepped in it.

June 17

After his shift ended at midnight, Ennis drove down to the Quill & Scroll. He found Penelope sitting at the end of the bar.

"Where's the sensitive conversationalist?"

"I broke up with him," she said, turning halfway toward him.

"What happened?"

She turned to fully face him now, revealing a blackened right eye.

"He did that?"

She smiled wanly.

"Where does this fuck live?"

"Forget it, George. It's over and there's no real harm."

Ennis pounded on the bar with his clenched right hand. "I wanna break that fucker's arms."

"Just forget it, George. You don't have to slay Penelope's suitor."

Ennis ordered a double shot of Windsor and a Schmidt's draft and turned back to her. "I missed you," he said quietly.

Ennis surprised himself by blurting that out. He had never said that to a woman.

Penelope smiled and touched his cheek.

"Wanna go down to the Melrose and get something to eat?" he asked.

At the venerable, 24-hour diner in South Philadelphia whose radio ad said that "Everyone who knows goes to Melrose," they ordered breakfast and talked shop.

"The Bully Pulpit isn't a bad place to work," Penelope was saying. "It would be even better if the owner didn't play grab-ass with the help."

"What do you do when he pulls that?"

"I tell him if he doesn't stop, I'm going to call his wife."

"Do you want me to mug him when he leaves work?"

"No," Penelope replied. She smiled then, ruefully, and added, "In my business, that sort of shit just comes with the territory."

Ennis winced at that and fell silent for a moment. Then, he told her about the press dinner the night before, at which he had sat at a table with Police Commissioner Frank Rizzo and listened to his storytelling.

A bear of a man at 6-2, 260, Rizzo was a commanding presence, charismatic, charming, and equipped with Joe Namath's self-promotional savvy. Already a Philadelphia fable by 1969, he exuded toughness during an American moment rife with socio-political ferment. And the way he dispensed that toughness in one of the nation's largest urban cauldrons was very polarizing.

Blue-collar whites who felt their neighborhoods threatened by black crime and occupation saw him as an almost messianic figure. Indeed, in South Philadelphia, where he grew up on Rosewood Street, he was The Nazarene.

On the other hand, blacks and white liberals, mindful of the humiliating outdoor strip searches he conducted on African American radicals, saw him as a racist.

The truth, of course, lay somewhere between devil and deity.

The devil/deity also often had an unexpected effect on women who came into his presence. Even if they had despised him from a distance, they often found him quite disarming in the flesh.

Ennis leaned over the booth table and began. "So, Rizzo's sitting there, pulling on a bottle of Bud and talking about the racial problem at Bok Vocational High School. You know, how the whites were attacking the black kids who had to pass through their neighborhood to get to the school.

"Frank says: 'So, fights would break out and we'd have to go in. And every time, after we got things calmed down, this kid would show up at the school and make a speech that would rile up the whites all over again. So, when he showed up yet again, I took him behind a paddy wagon and gave him two quick shots to the gut. He didn't make any more speeches after that.'"

Penelope pursed her lips in disbelief. "He says something like that in front of reporters? He's that sure he won't be quoted?"

"In a context like that, guys sitting around drinking beer, reporters consider stuff like that off the record. But in his case, I think it's more than that. I think it's also fear."

"Are you afraid of him?"

Ennis made a tent with his fingers. "I could say that since the man's got three inches and 80 pounds on me, I wouldn't be too interested in duking it out with him. But, it's not just his size that's intimidating, it's not knowing what he's capable of."

"So, you'd be afraid to write it."

"It's really academic. The *Public Sentinel*'s editor wouldn't let it in the paper, anyway. I mean, he and Rizzo have a weekly lunch in a private club."

Later, on the sidewalk outside Penelope's studio: "Well, thank you for joining me this evening," Ennis said, stroking her left cheek. "Perhaps we could have dinner tomorrow night."

"What?"

"I'm suggesting we could have dinner, at Arthur's Steak House if you'd like."

"George, this sudden burst of civility? Have you been watching English television shows?"

"Does Benny Hill count?"

"Well, why don't we go in and let you get back in character?"

"I don't think so. I want the record to show that we had a stand-alone conversation and went on to dinner the next evening."

"George, for god's sake. You're a sweet boy and I want you to come in."

"No, it's important that I make this point." He kissed her then, and started off toward his Camaro.

June 18

Janet leaned back in her white leather sofa, took a big swig from her glass of Stoli, and called Ennis.

"Can Georgie Porgie come out to play?" she asked, huskily.

"I'm sick in bed, throwing up and spending a lot of time in the bathroom. 'Fraid I'll have to take a rain check."

June 19

It was 9:45 p.m. and Ennis was finishing a nine-inch obit for the B when Harrigan called him to the city desk. Ennis thought the night city editor's summons was a bit clipped, even edgy.

"Let's go in Lawson's lair," Harrigan said, motioning toward the empty office of Managing Editor James L. Lawson.

Harrigan took Lawson's chair and motioned to one on the other side of the desk.

"Someone heard you talking about sleeping with a movie actress you interviewed. Is that true?"

Ennis felt nauseous. Obviously, someone had been listening when he told Bill Guest about the sexual encounter while the two men were sitting at the bar in the Quill & Scroll earlier in the week. He wouldn't even have told his best friend if he hadn't been half in the bag.

"Yeah, it's true."

"Who was it?"

"Cassandra Mitchell."

"I remember the interview. You did it when you were on loan to the entertainment department.

"Listen, George. There's an old saying in our business: If you cover the circus, you don't fuck the elephants. And you've been a newspaperman long enough to know that."

Ennis stared at the desk top, then looked up at Harrigan. "I have no excuse, sir. I don't know what I was thinking."

"It's really not what you were thinking, it's what you were thinking with—namely, your other head."

Ennis's face drooped into his left hand. Harrigan paused egregiously to let him squirm and then said: "Fortunately for you, I think you're a promising newsman who's worth a second chance. And even more fortunately for you, the guy who heard you is a friend of mine who will keep his mouth shut.

"But, don't you ever pull a trick like that again. Because if you do and I find out about it, I'm going to kick your ass down the stairs and that will be it. This isn't the *Inquirer* or the *Daily News*, you know. There's no Newspaper Guild here to save your job. Understood?"

"Yes, sir."

"Okay, get back to work. And stop sir-ing me."

Later, Ennis and Guest stopped at the Quill & Scroll. Ennis told his friend about his conversation with Harrigan.

"Yeah, well," Guest responded. "I guess it's not a good idea to dip your pen in the story subject's inkwell, and an even worse idea to talk about it."

June 20

Horst Dietrich parked his 1964 Ferrari 275 GTB coupe a block from Fitler Square. The car's freshly waxed arrest-me red finish gleamed in the pale of a streetlight as it disgorged its tall, angular occupant—and the canvas bag he was carrying. Dietrich glanced at the Patek Philippe on his left wrist. It was 9:25 p.m.

The thunderstorm was over. Dietrich stepped off the curb into the streetlight's dominion, walked across the rain-polished street to the square, then turned toward the trash can Guest had designated. It was rather dark in the square, and Dietrich was confident no one had seen him drop the bag in the can, although he felt the blackmailer may well have seen him approaching. He walked on about 50 yards, then crossed the street as if to return to his car.

Guest watched as Dietrich departed the square. He waited a few minutes after Dietrich passed out of view, then moved in to retrieve the bag. He walked back to his 1963 Ford Falcon station wagon, which was hunched in the shadows nursing the dings, rusty scratches, and other urban indignities that had left it with such a severe case of automotive acne. He opened the bag and leafed through the packs of $100 bills. It seemed like it was all there. He'd make sure when he got home. He dropped the research notes and salacious negatives in a mail box on the way back to his apartment.

What Guest didn't know was that Dietrich had doubled back to the square, crouched behind a parked car, and got a good look at him when he crossed the well-lighted street, carrying the canvas bag.

MIAMI, FL
June 22
Osvaldo Gagliardi was sitting in his expansive office on Miami's Brickell Avenue, doing due diligence on his latest corporate target. Gagliardi was ahead of his time. Long before terms like leveraged buyout and arbitrage entered the popular vocabulary, Ozzie was making a fortune by butchering businesses and putting breadwinners out of work.

He had a formula. He would look for a multi-division corporation whose unprofitable nuclear business was negating the good results from its relatively revenue-rich satellites. After he and his fellow investors gained control of the company, the consortium would sell off the profitable satellites to service debt. Next, Gagliardi et al would sic a top-notch cost-cutter on the core business. By dramatically slashing overhead, largely by trimming the work force, Gagliardi and his partners would put the company in the black, then sell it for a good profit before the cuts had any chance to erode its viability.

Among the uses for his hypertrophic fortune was the acquisition of exotic sports cars and a procession of lovely young mistresses with monetary needs as considerable as their breast implants. Those needs included an expensive apartment, which he conveniently rented near his Miami office.

Life was good. Fast Ferraris and fast foxes. But the 58-year-old Gagliardi did have one problem: a 48-year-old wife who had had a gutful of his serial adultery.

As Gagliardi was pressing a fiscal stethoscope against the chest of his next corporate prey, his wife, Marjorie, was lying in a hotel bed 20 miles from her Miami Beach home. Her 32-year-old lover, Carlos Martinez, was by her side, idly trying to elicit an erection from her left nipple.

Martinez had been a fringe player in the Philadelphia mob and wasn't in line for any promotions since he wasn't of Italian descent. So, he had recently migrated to Miami, where organized crime was less Italo-centric.

"Carlos, do you know anyone in Philadelphia who could arrange a hit?" Mrs. Gaglilardi asked, matter-of-factly.

"What?"

"You heard me."

Martinez looked at her quizzically. "You aren't thinking what I think you're thinking, are you?"

Her small smile was contagious.

"Okay. I'll make a call, somebody will call you, somebody will buy the farm, and the good times will roll. Vegas, here we come."

Martinez smiled broadly. Mrs. Gagliardi did not.

June 24

Martinez telephoned Antonio Bonafucci, who owed him a favor. (Martinez and a colleague had discouraged a South Philadelphia punk from dating Bonafucci's daughter by working him over and then nipping the tips off two of his fingers with sheet-metal shears.) He told Bonafucci that his rich girlfriend wanted to unload her hubby.

The mob underboss told him he would pass along his request to someone who could take care of the matter.

Bonafucci phoned his hit broker, who called Mrs. Gagliardi and asked for the name of the quarry, as well as the latter's home and business addresses. She gave him the information for her husband.

And her lover.

Dietrich wasn't the only person who despised loose ends.

The broker got off the phone with Mrs. Gagliardi and called Mako. He told Dietrich that the double hit would mean $10,000 ($70,521 in 2021 dollars) for him and that the customer wanted the work done as soon as possible. Dietrich said the kills would have to wait until the week of the 29th because of a previous engagement.

The previous engagement, of course, was dealing with Bill Guest. The initial phase of the solution to the Guest problem was pretty straightforward: Get into the newsroom clerk's safety deposit box and grab those pictures and research notes.

June 25

It was 9:15 a.m. Dietrich parked a half-block from Guest's walk-up near 10th and South. He had driven here in his sister's anonymous Ford Fairlane sedan. His Ferrari would have been a rather incongruous presence in this gray, gritty border country between Center City and South Philadelphia, where South Street's cheap rents had engendered a vibrant artist colony and encouraged continued occupation by old neighborhood clothing stores like Krass Brothers, "Store of the Stars." (Benny Krass's slogan was, "If you didn't get your suit at Krass Brothers, you was robbed." A banty rooster of a man, Benny drove a yellow Rolls-Royce and starred in local TV ads that featured menopausal blondes in succinct swim wear.)

Dietrich, who had disguised himself with a realistic fake beard, sunglasses, and a Phillies cap, found Guest's world-weary Falcon wagon parked nearby on Bainbridge Street. Seeing no one around, he pulled a slim-jim from his briefcase and pushed its thin blade down alongside the window of the front passenger's door until it encountered the locking mechanism, which he manipulated to unlock the door.

It was now 9:30. Figuring Guest would be along shortly (he had to be to work by 10:00), Dietrich walked to a curbside sycamore, a few feet from the back of the Falcon. He leaned against the tree, on the side opposite Guest's imminent approach, and lit a cigarette. He spotted the approaching Guest a few minutes later, about 40 yards away. He ducked back, stepped on his cigarette, and waited for the sound of the door opening. Dietrich emerged from behind the tree at precisely the moment Guest bent over to get in. He walked briskly to the passenger's side, opened the unlocked door with his right hand, and got in, pulling his .45 from a jacket pocket with his left hand as he did so.

"Good morning, Mr. Guest."

"What the hell!" Guest responded.

"You and I are going to your bank now, to get my money and whatever else might be in your safety deposit box," Dietrich said, transferring the gun from his left hand to his right.

"Your money?"

"Don't get cute. I want that blackmail money."

"You're accusing me of blackmailing you?"

"Don't seem so surprised, Mr. Guest. Surely you suspected yourself."

Guest slumped back in the driver's seat, but his shoulders didn't sag in defeat.

"I'm not taking you to the bank, and I'm not giving you shit!" Guest said. "And if you kill me, the envelope will be opened, and the police will see the sex prints and my research on your business trips."

"Oh, Mr. Guest, I didn't want to have to play this card. It's so gauche, so ungentlemanly. But the fact is, if we don't visit your savings account and your safety deposit box right now, I'm going to have to visit your beloved sister and niece in Sewell, N.J. Your sister would die immediately, but your niece would cross the River Styx only after participating in a scientific experiment, an experiment in which we see what happens when you penetrate a 12-year-old vagina with a mature male member."

"You sick fuck!" Guest yelled. He then placed his face in his hands. Finally, he said, "So, that's the deal: I keep them alive by giving you the money and pictures—and sign my own death warrant in the process."

"*Au contraire*, Mr. Guest. I don't think you'll be talking to anyone under the circumstances, so there's no real reason for your demise. Now, let's be off to the bank."

Dietrich leaned back and grimaced. He was repulsed by the Falcon's old car smell. He always kept two evergreen-shaped air fresheners in his Ferrari.

Later that Wednesday, at 5:45 p.m., Harry Ralston left the newsroom to drink his dinner at a bar behind the paper called Freddie's Filling Station. "Highball Harry," as the news staff called him behind his back, was the *Public Sentinel*'s wire room clerk, and the scion of a wealthy Main Line family. He was chauffeured to work each day in his parents' Bentley. He got on the payroll, despite his alcoholism, because Martin Grimsley, the paper's editor, had promised his father, a country club buddy, that he would give him a job. After telling the city editor that he was going to hire Highball, he pointed out that Ralston shouldn't be a problem because his job was almost too simple to screw up. All he had to do was tear stories off the wire machines, deliver them to the operations desk, and bring early copies of the A edition to operations and the city desk.

At 6:15, Harrigan called Freddie's and got Highball on the phone.

"Harry, where are my copies of the A?"

"I'm working on it, I'm working on it," Highball replied irritably before hanging up.

Later that evening, Ennis walked into the men's room near the city desk. Larry Arabis's combat jacket was draped over a stall door along with his shirt, pants, and underwear. His sock-stuffed combat boots stood at attention beneath the door.

Ennis was standing at a urinal when a low moan emanated from the stall. He looked over his shoulder to see Arabis's heels rhythmically rise in unison, then drop back to the floor.

Presently, Ennis walked back to his typewriter. At the adjacent desk, Lansky was watching Levandowski installing a hasp on the top drawer of his desk to stop the pilfering once and for all.

"I just witnessed a strange, pagan ritual," Ennis told Lansky. "Arabis was apparently naked in a toilet stall, moaning and chanting. Could he be a druid? Was he going to emerge from the stall and sacrifice a gerbil?"

"Obviously, something holy was happening there," Lansky concluded, stroking his chin. "Maybe he's the Mystery Shitter and he was blessing his package."

June 26

Tomaso Baldini, a *Public Sentinel* assistant sports editor, was lolling back in his office chair, holding court with two copy boys.

"Making the playoffs in the NHL doesn't involve a lot of heavy lifting," he was saying. "They play a 76-game schedule to eliminate a couple root cellar residents like the Pittsburgh Penguins and the Minnesota North Stars. I mean, the (Philadelphia) Flyers got in the playoffs this year after winning 20 of their 76 games."

Jim Crowley, the sports editor, came up behind Baldini and dropped a Horst Dietrich column on his desk for editing.

"Maybe if I give you something to do, Mr. Baldini, these busy copy boys could get back to work," Crowley said.

Baldini started reading the column.

"Aw, shit, it's his annual minor league baseball turd," Baldini announced to the desk denizens around him. "It's the same fuckin' column every summer: the four-hour bus rides, the greasy spoon hamburgers, the shared $10 motel rooms. And yet, they keep hustling, keep dreaming the dream of being called up to The Show.

"I'm going to be fucking ill."

Early that evening, Guest returned from work to find his apartment ransacked. He also found Dietrich rising from behind the overturned sofa with a .22 caliber revolver in his hand.

"Have a seat," Dietrich said, motioning toward a well-worn easy chair. "You know, you're going to have to do something about security," he added. "That lock was awfully easy to pick."

He smiled and continued. "Well, Mr. Guest, I spent the past hour-and-a-half looking for more prints and more copies of your detective work. Guess there aren't any."

"No, there aren't."

Dietrich picked up a throw pillow lying on the sofa. "Well, I suppose it's time to end this sordid affair—and what better setting than your tacky apartment?"

Guest stared at him incredulously. Dietrich responded: "You didn't really expect me to let you live, did you?"

"I wasn't sure."

Terror had incarcerated Guest. Then, suddenly, he was released from fear's custody. A liberating triumvirate of defiance, anger, and resignation took charge of him.

"My apartment isn't nearly as tacky as your sex life," Guest said. "What could be tackier than licking your kid sister's pussy?"

Dietrich suddenly stepped forward and fired.

He had brought the small-caliber revolver because he didn't want to make a lot of noise. To further minimize the risk of being heard, he had pushed the muzzle of the .22-caliber pistol into the sound-deadening pillow in his left hand before discharging it. The bullet he fired was the nastiest .22 of them all: a long rifle hollow point. The bullet mushroomed when it struck the formidable bone in Guest's forehead, then recruited brain tissue as it migrated to the back of his skull. A second shot nicked a rib, passed near his heart, and exited the thoracic cavity. Failing to encounter enough resistance to significantly deform a hollow point, the second bullet came to rest in the chair back's padding virtually unscathed. Guest was mortally wounded and unconscious, but Dietrich was leaving nothing to chance. He opened a six-inch switchblade and slit the little man's throat, severing both carotid arteries in the process. Guest was dead for nearly two minutes by the time Dietrich had closed the apartment building's front door and removed his latex gloves.

June 27

Seth Menges, the day city editor, had called Guest's apartment several times when he failed to show up for work at 10:30.

"This isn't like Guest," he said to an assistant editor named Hal Framington. "He'd have called if he were sick. Hal, call whoever's covering the Roundhouse (police headquarters) and ask him to request a police check on him."

The police reporter called back 70 minutes later.

"A uniform found him in his apartment. He was shot in the head and chest and his throat was cut. The place was turned upside down."

Ennis came in a short time later to start his 1:00 to 9:00 p.m. shift. Menges told him what had happened.

"Oh no!" Ennis said, pressing his hands to his temples. "Not Bill, not Bill."

He dropped heavily into Menges's chair and stared vacantly at the editor's copy spike. He absently rubbed its sharp point with his thumb. He looked up, finally, with wet eyes. "Do they have the guy?" he asked Menges.

"No."

"I'd like to take a week off if it's okay with you and Denny."

"I'm sure that'll be fine, George," Menges replied. "But listen. Go home and take it easy. Don't try to play detective. Let Homicide do its job."

Ennis got in his Camaro and headed down to Guest's apartment, near 10th and South. A uniform was stationed at the building entrance.

Ennis showed him his press card.

"That's a crime scene. You know you can't go in there."

"Who's in charge of the investigation?" Ennis asked.

"Kerry Shoustal."

Shoustal was a top homicide detective whom Ennis had got to know during his year as a police reporter. They had become friends and sometimes met for a drink after work.

"Could someone ask him if George Ennis could come up?"

The detective looked up from his perusal of the papers on the floor next to an end table when Ennis walked in.

"Rudy Steinmetz already got the story," Shoustal said. "So, what are you doing here?"

"He was a good friend."

Shoustal sighed. "Alright. you can stay if you don't touch anything." Guest's body had already been removed, leaving behind an amorphous stain where he had bled on a faux oriental rug. A detective was gingerly going through the scattered papers and other debris, looking for something that could help. Another was dusting door knobs and furniture for fingerprints.

"So, what happened, Kerry?"

"I think somebody tossed the place, and then shot your friend when he came home from work. But this situation doesn't feel like your usual break-in. First of all, burglars generally prefer more upmarket hunting grounds than 10th and South. Second, if the intruder were here to boost valuables, he would have taken more than your friend's wallet. He would have grabbed the watches and the other jewelry in the dresser drawer. But, he didn't. That, and the sheer extent of the ransacking, makes me think he was looking for something else.

"And then, there's the killing itself. If someone walks in on you while you're robbing their home, you might panic and take a shot at them before you run out. But in this case, the killer used a pillow to muffle the sound of a shot fired at point-blank range into Mr. Guest's forehead and chest. He then slit his throat.

"So, I don't think this was some spur-of-the-moment thing. This was an execution."

Shoustal paused. "Can you think of something he knew, something he had that might cause someone to want him dead?"

Ennis shook his head. "I can't imagine why anyone would want to kill him," he said.

"Well, if you think of anything, call me," Shoustal said, and started toward the detective going through the papers on the floor. Ennis nodded, thrust his hands into his pockets, and headed for the door. He paused en route and turned to Shoustal.

"You know, he did recently give me a key to his safety deposit box. I was to open it in the event of his death."

"Do you want to give me that key?" Shoustal asked. "I'll take a look."

Ennis took the key from his wallet and handed it to the detective.

As Ennis approached the entrance to his apartment building, grief and anger sparred in his head, taking turns getting the upper hand. Penelope was sitting on the front steps, waiting for him. In the ensuing years, the sadness and compassion in her eyes would remain forever fresh.

"I heard about Bill on the radio," she said, rising and putting her arms around him. "I'm sorry, George. I'm so sorry."

Up in his apartment, Ennis leaned over the chrome and Formica kitchen table he had bought at a used furniture store in South Philadelphia and poured himself a second double shot of blended Canadian whiskey. He downed it and chased it with a swig of Pabst Blue Ribbon. His eyes were red-rimmed. He blotted the tears with the cuffs of his shirt.

"Bill was really more than my best friend," he said. "In ways, he was the brother I never had and the father I could really talk to. He was a vocational role model, a mentor. He taught me so much.

"God, I loved that guy."

Penelope stroked his hair. "I know you did, dear. Now, why don't you lie down and try to get a little rest?"

NEW YORK, NY
June 28
The Stonewall Inn was a crummy but popular mob-run gay bar on Christopher Street in New York City's Greenwich Village when the historic riots broke out there in the early morning hours on this date.

The bar was usually tipped off by corrupt police when a raid was imminent, but not this time. Policemen entered the bar, roughed up customers, and arrested 13, including employees and patrons who had violated the state's gender-appropriate clothing law. (Policewomen checked out suspected cross-dressers in the bathroom.)

Sick and tired of the constant harassment, angered by the manhandling, a mob began tossing stones and bottles at the cops. In a matter of minutes, hundreds of people were rioting. The police barricaded themselves and several prisoners in the bar, which the rioters tried to set on fire. (Firemen extinguished the flames.)

Protesters, sometimes thousands strong, continued to demonstrate in the area for five more days, and their efforts, while they didn't mark the birth of the gay rights movement, proved a catalyst for the burgeoning LGBT activism that followed. In 2016, President Obama declared the inn and its surroundings a national monument.

PHILADELPHIA, PA
Same day
Ennis awoke well after the riot had started some 90 miles away. He had needed quite a few shots and beers to get to sleep. He awoke with an ache in his head—and his heart. He drank coffee, read the *Public Sentinel* account of his friend's murder, and watched the TV news reports.

At 11:30, he called Shoustal to see if there were any breaks in the case.

"The uniforms are bringing in someone who tried to buy a Rolex at Bailey, Banks & Biddle with one of Guest's credit cards."

"May I come down and talk to you after you question him?"

"Sure."

The patrolmen brought the suspect to an interrogation room at the Roundhouse. Shoustal sat down at a table opposite Malcolm Kerr, who was 51, unemployed, and wearing the new suit, tie, shirt, and shoes purchased at Wanamaker's with Guest's credit card.

"Gee, Malcolm, you look great," Shoustal said. "That Rolex would have made you look even better. Too bad the clerk at Bailey, Banks & Biddle recognized Bill Guest's name from this morning's stories about his murder."

"Where do you live, Malcolm?"

"Here and there. I'm sort of between residences at the moment."

"Where'd you get the cards?"

"Listen, I know my rights. I don't have to talk to you until my attorney gets here."

"Gosh, Malcolm, you must watch a lot of police shows on television when you aren't between residences. But, you're right, you don't have to talk to me until your counselor arrives. You can wait in a cell. So, I'm going to have Lamar share his cell with you. Lamar is a 350-pound bull faggot who would like to redesign your asshole. I don't know if he has any sexually transmitted diseases at the moment, but I do believe his legendary schwanz is going to leave you with a rather tender poop chute."

"You wouldn't!"

"Oh, but I would, and you better hope Lamar is feeling sociable enough to merely remodel your rectum. If he's in an anti-social funk, he just might gouge out one of your eyes and use the socket for a good old-fashioned skull fuck."

"You put me in there, and I'll report you to the ACLU!"

"What, and tell 'em that I respected your rights by waiting until your public defender arrived?"

Kerr slumped in his chair and rubbed his forehead. "Alright. I ducked into an alley near 9th and Bainbridge to take a piss and saw the wallet. There was no money in it, but there were some credit cards. I used one to buy the clothes and wanted to use the other to get an expensive watch I could hock. That would've solved my financial problems for a while."

Ennis was waiting for Shoustal outside the interrogation room.

"This guy told me he found Guest's wallet in an alley, then used one credit card to buy clothes and tried to use another to purchase a Rolex. I think he's telling the truth. He's in custody on the card capers, but I don't think he's our boy. He's just your standard Center City kookadoo."

"Did you get a chance to check Bill's safety deposit box," Ennis asked.

"Yeah. It was empty, and I found that rather strange. The man had something in that safety deposit box he wanted you to see in the event of his death, and yet it was empty. I was left wondering if that box had been emptied for the same reason his apartment was ransacked.

"A bank officer gave your friend access to his box on Wednesday. He told me he was accompanied by someone: a tall man with a beard, sunglasses, a Phillies cap—and a limp. Does that ring a bell?"

"No one I can think of," Ennis replied.

"I hate to say this George, I know the guy was your friend, but I can't help thinking he was trying to shake somebody down. It's the only explanation that makes any sense at this point."

"Kerry, I can see how what we know might lead you to this place. But the Bill Guest I knew had a reputation as a scrupulous reporter, and I saw him as a man with a moral compass. I can't imagine him blackmailing somebody."

Shoustal dropped his head, rubbed his forehead, and let his unseen eyes roll back. He said nothing.

June 30
On the way to work this Monday afternoon, Lansky had a vision. It

wasn't exactly like the one that Paul had on the road to Damascus. He had come up with a way to purloin Levandowski's goods, even though the crime-fighting newsman had now installed hefty hasps and padlocks on both of his desk drawers.

When Levandowski and Harrigan had gone out for dinner, Lansky, with the help of a copy boy, had pulled out the unused desk abutting Levandowski's, thus exposing the back of Boris's newsroom Fort Knox. The sheet steel back panel behind the drawers was secured to the desk with sheet-metal screws. Lansky backed out the 16 screws and lifted the panel out of the way, exposing the two drawers. He then reached in and removed the contents of both drawers. Finally, he replaced the panel and he and the copy boy pushed the adjacent desk back in place.

Levandowski discovered the theft shortly after he returned from dinner and became hysterical.

"Listen, Boris," Harrigan said. "We're going to find out where your goods are and who stole them. This will not stand. So calm down. We're going to get to the bottom of this, and the guilty person or persons will be held accountable.

"Okay, everybody who's done their work for the B, help us look for Boris's goods." Then, under his breath, he told Lansky to come with him.

"Lansky, I know you did this. Now, where's his shit?"

"It's in the closet next to Lawson's office."

The two checked desks and filing cabinets as they gradually made their way toward the managing editor's office.

"Lansky, when you get older and achieve adolescence, perhaps you'll grasp the meaning of 'enough is enough.' I mean, it was funny the first time."

"I thought it was pretty funny the second time," Lansky countered.

"Saul, this guy is a real whack-O-matic. If he gets exercised enough, he just might defenestrate—you know, go up to the 20th floor and do a half gainer out a window. I don't want to be part of that, so this has to end right now. We are going to give his crap back and I am going to tell him that I will investigate this matter until I find the guilty party. Two days from now, I will tell him that I have found the perpetrator and that that person is very contrite and disgusted with himself, and wants to make reparations in the amount of $100 on the condition that he is spared the humiliation of being identified."

"In other words, I'm to be fined $100 for an act of comedic genius."

"Yep. And you don't even want to think about what happens to those who don't pay their fines. I mean, do you realize how many boondock burgs in the hinterlands have sewer authorities whose meetings are covered by our stringers? In the past, I've tried to spread those stories around, share the misery, but there's no reason why one rewrite man couldn't become the *Public Sentinel*'s sewer specialist."

"Denny, I think I liked you better when you just pulled the wings off butterflies."

July 1

It was Tuesday, a week since Guest's death. It had been a draining week. Ennis had taken his dead friend's sister, Beth, to the funeral home, where the owner's son had treated her with theatrical respect and concern and tried to sell her a brass-trimmed, satin-upholstered mahogany coffin she couldn't afford. The practiced pitch, at the confluence of dramaturgy and capitalism, left Ennis somewhere between annoyance and anger.

The burial, attended only by Guest's sister, niece, and Ennis, was on Monday. Now, on Tuesday morning, Ennis was about to drive over to Sewell, N.J., to help Beth plan a memorial service that would include his friend's minuscule family and a much more ample corps of colleagues. But first, he did what he did every morning since Guest's death: He called Detective Shoustal to see if there were any developments in the investigation.

"Nothing new," Shoustal said. "We have yet to find anyone who saw a stranger going in or out of his apartment house," Shoustal said.

"Sounds like this case is going cold on us, Kerry."

"It could well be, George, but we'll keep trying."

"Thanks."

Ennis drove over to Sewell and pulled into the gravel driveway of Guest's sister's modest frame rancher. Beth Guest-Mumford answered the door. She looked up at him with loss-haunted eyes.

They took seats in the living room. She thought Monday evening, July 7, would be a good time for the memorial service, and Old Swedes' Church would be a good place. She said Guest, while an agnostic, had always admired the South Philadelphia church, which had been built at the dawn of the 18th Century. He liked to wander among the gravestones in its contiguous cemetery, many of which had been rendered illegible by time's corrosive vandalism. Also, Ennis thought his friend would like the fact that the priest was known to "minister" to the flock hanging out in Dirty Frank's bar and wasn't too stringent on religious orthodoxy.

Ennis said he would see if the Episcopal church and its priest would be available on that following Monday. He also asked her what she wanted to do about her brother's possessions.

"I know this is an imposition," she replied, "but could you deal with them? I just don't want to go in there."

"Of course."

On his drive back to the city, it occurred to Ennis that after a week of dwelling constantly on his friend's death and his grief, the weight on his spiritual shoulders was beginning to lighten. He felt a sense of normalcy seeping back into his life. He wasn't as depressed. He felt a little guilty for feeling this way, for thinking again about making love to Penelope.

That night, on the occasion of her 26th birthday, he took Penelope down to 7th and Bainbridge for dinner at an upmarket restaurant called The Saloon. Afterward, they went back to her apartment where they made love for the first time in more than a week.

Ennis rolled off her and lay on his back, staring at the ceiling. "I'm 27," he said. "How old is your ex-boyfriend?"

"Twenty-eight."

"And until today, you were only 25."

"What are you getting at?" she asked.

"That you obviously have a thing for older men."

"Well, I do," she said with a straight face. "They are more experienced, more worldly than younger males. They are more thoughtful, too, and they aren't so preoccupied with sex. After one or two rolls in the hay, they'll just go to sleep or discuss the theological implications of The Second Law of Thermodynamics. They won't greedily seek *número tres.*"

"If I were to let history repeat itself, and greedily pursue *número tres,* would you dismiss me as 27 going on 18?"

"You're not going to get a chance to find out because I'm taking a nap."

MIAMI, FL

July 2

Since no reasonable sports column fodder had presented itself in Miami, Dietrich had taken two weeks of vacation to fly down here for the Gagliardi/Martinez hit. He didn't want to hurry the prep work. He wanted adequate time for each surveillance and kill.

He had started with Gagliardi on June 29, the day after his arrival. He had found Gagliardi was very much a man of routine. Each morning, at 9 o'clock, he would put the top down on his beloved 1959 Ferrari 250 GT California Spyder SWB and drive from his Miami Beach home to his office in downtown Miami, where he would park in the building's ground-level garage.

Dietrich had ascertained the location of Gagliardi's parking space and was standing by it, pretending to be locking the contiguous car, when his quarry pulled in. He drew his .45 as Gagliardi shut down the Ferrari. The corporate raider saw only the big gun. He didn't notice the latex glove on the hand holding it.

"What the hell is this?" Gagliardi exclaimed.

"It's about money, Mr. Gagliardi."

With his gun trained on the driver, Dietrich came around to the passenger side and got in.

"Let's put the top up, Mr. Gagliardi, and then we'll have a little chat."

When the roof was up, Dietrich told him to turn to the side and put his hands behind his back. After handcuffing Gagliardi, Dietrich looked around the garage. Seeing no one, he reached inside the plastic bag in his sport coat pocket and produced a chloroform-soaked wash cloth which he pressed against Gagliardi's mouth. Gagliardi reflexively inhaled, and that was the beginning of the end for the smaller man. He struggled at the outset, but then weakened and went limp.

Dietrich removed the handcuffs, which he had padded to prevent possible wrist bruising, and re-positioned the unconscious man behind the wheel. Seeing no one else in the garage, he placed in Gagliardi's right hand the wiped-clean .38-caliber revolver he had purchased in a pawn shop.

Getting gunpowder residue on Gagliardi's right hand and sleeve was as important as getting his fingerprints on the gun. So, holding Gagliardi's right hand on the gun handle with his left hand, Dietrich raised the weapon and placed its muzzle against the victim's right temple.

He then used his right hand to push Gagliardi's finger back against the trigger. The weapon discharged. The bullet exited the other side of Gagliardi's head, spraying blood and bone on the driver's side window and door panel, as well as the inside of the convertible top.

Dietrich took a last look around the car's interior. There was still no one else in the garage, so he quickly pulled off the gloves and made his way to the stairway. He climbed to the fourth floor, took the elevator down to the lobby, and left the building.

PHILADELPHIA, PA

Still July 2

When Ennis arrived in the newsroom at 5:00 p.m., he found a crestfallen Lansky sitting at his desk.

"Saul, what's up?"

"I just walked out on my wife."

I'm sorry to hear that."

"Well, it's been coming for a while, as you know. Anyway, I'm going to stay in a hotel tonight. Do you think Father Donovan has any lodgings?"

"He usually does."

"Father Donovan" was Pete Donovan, a *Public Sentinel* copy editor who rented rooms in his large, old house in the city's Germantown section to separated newsmen. His place was known in the newsroom as Father Donovan's Home for Wayward Boys.

In the wake of Ennis's arrival, Highball Harry brought up copies of the A edition. Night city editor Harrigan started reading through the local news stories on the A's B page, making corrections. The "fixes" on this "marker page" would then be sent down to the composing room for inclusion in the subsequent B edition.

Among the chief fixes on the B page would be the stitching of the grievous literary wounds inflicted by Charles Sumner, the paper's city hall bureau chief.

Sumner was not a source of warm and fuzzy feelings in the newsroom. He was nastier than a junkyard Doberman on a 200-calorie diet. If anyone said anything nice about someone, Sumner would quickly develop an antidote for the compliment—such as, "He cheats at cards."

And then there was his approach to his job. To impress management, Sumner frequently would try to cover two city hall meetings held at the same time, popping in and out of the two sessions and winding up with two half-assed stories.

His writing made matters worse. Sumner didn't so much write a story as make war on his typewriter. Composing a story for him was a matter of pistol-whipping the keys and grimacing a lot. Lansky once observed that if he had to suffer that much to write a story, he would rather pump out septic tanks.

The result of all that suffering was prose of a density beyond mere opacity. The day city editor didn't usually have time to deal with the Sumner gibberish for the A, so it would fall on the night city editor to have a rewrite man de-code it for the B.

Harrigan looked up balefully from Sumner's B page center piece on a City Planning Commission meeting, which was laid out like the Philadelphia telephone directory but was much less interesting, and said: "Okay, whose turn is it to rewrite Sumner?"

Ennis squirmed and then said, "I guess it's mine."

Harrigan glanced back at the Sumner piece disgustedly and said, "I have a better idea." He then squeezed the B page marker into a ball and tossed it in his trashcan—and Sumner's story never appeared after the A.

July 3

Enraged by the fate of his story, Sumner charged into the newsroom at 10:30 a.m. and screamed a lot. Menges, the day city editor, finally suggested that the gentleman from the city hall bureau should go fuck himself.

That afternoon, prior to his 4:00 to midnight shift, Ennis stopped in at Shoustal's office at the Roundhouse to check on the Guest investigation.

"Nothing much," Shoustal said. "We did talk to a man who lives in the neighborhood who saw a tall male stranger walking near Guest's apartment building on the evening of the killing. He didn't give us much of a description, though."

"Did he notice if he had a beard?" Ennis asked.

"He said he didn't," Shoustal replied.

MIAMI, FL
July 4

Dietrich put down that morning's *Miami Herald* and smiled. The police were calling Gagliardi's death an apparent suicide, just as he had planned.

Martinez's death would not require as much stagecraft. It wouldn't demand as much research, either, thanks to the detective hired earlier by the cautious Mrs. Gagliardi. The detective's report, which a courier had handed to Dietrich at a bus top, said that in addition to sleeping with his middle-aged paramour twice a week (a practice she put on hold after her husband's death), Martinez had a 22-year-old girlfriend on the side. The detective reported that Martinez would visit her in the evening, on days when Mrs. Gagliardi didn't require his afternoon essence. He'd leave his apartment about 9:00 p.m., then walk seven blocks to hers, where he'd spend the night.

This evening, at 9:05, on the most deserted leg of Martinez's walk to his girlfriend's apartment, Dietrich stepped out of an alley as his victim passed and hit him on the back of the head with the lug wrench from his rental car. He pulled the unconscious man into the alley and struck his head two more times. Feeling no pulse, he then took Martinez's watch and wallet to suggest robbery.

An hour later, he was seated in an elite French restaurant, where his $30 bill ($212.00 in 2021 dollars) included a prime, aged entrecôte and an exceptional bottle of 12-year-old burgundy. He flew back to Philadelphia the next morning—first class.

PHILADELPHIA, PA
July 5

The police had finished with the Guest crime scene, and Ennis had reached a point where he felt he could face it. So, he had rented a van on this Saturday morning and driven to his dead friend's apartment.

The police had left the tossed apartment as they found it. Ennis picked up Guest's scattered papers and then went through them, looking for something that might help the stalled investigation. He found nothing.

After a bit of housekeeping, he dropped heavily into a leatherette recliner and surveyed the tidied apartment. The blood-stained faux oriental area rug was the only reminder that a murder had been committed here. Ennis sagged back in the chair and let the surf of sadness roll over him.

There was a knock at the door. Lansky had arrived to help him load up the furniture and clothing they would take to a Goodwill store.

Ennis kept Guest's walnut filing cabinet, a brass-trimmed 19th-century piece that one of the dead man's friends had picked up in Morocco while serving as a roving reporter for the *Los Angeles Guardian*. He had given Guest's sister the old newsman's watches and jewelry, so the antique cabinet and the mundane muddle of receipts and personal papers it contained was his only tangible connection to his best friend.

That evening, Ennis took Penelope to dinner at Dante & Luigi's, at 10th and Catharine in South Philadelphia. They went back to his place and watched television on the sofa. She cuddled against him while he stroked her hair.

"Do you think we should try to have a baby?" he asked.

She looked at him incredulously. "Aren't you putting the reproductive cart before the marital horse or something like that?"

"Not at all," he said, rising from the sofa and kneeling before her. "I am now making a formal request: Will you marry me?"

"George, this is so out of the blue. I don't know what to say."

"It's not out of the blue. You know I'm in love with you."

He glanced down, and then looked up at her again with soulful, beseeching eyes.

"So, I'm going to ask you again: Will you marry me?"

"George," she said, placing her hands on his cheeks, "how could I refuse when you look at me like that? Yes, I will."

"You've made me so happy," he said.

Penelope looked at his handsome face, into those riveting eyes as blue and deep as the Caribbean, and felt slightly lightheaded.

Ennis reached into his pocket, removed a quarter-carat diamond engagement ring, and placed it on her ring finger. Penelope bought into the timeless proposal liturgy with: "George, it's beautiful. I love it.

"But how did you know my ring size? It fits perfectly."

"Your co-worker, Rhonda, told me."

That night marked the first time Ennis didn't use a prophylactic.

July 6

Janet phoned Ennis. "George, it's been a while. I think you've been avoiding me. Hopefully, I'm wrong, and you can come over for a consultation."

"Janet, you're a wonderful, desirable woman and a dear friend, but I can't come over. The truth is, I'm now living with someone else."

"But that doesn't mean Georgie Porgie can't come out to play. It doesn't mean he can't sow the odd wild oat."

"Janet, I just proposed to the woman."

"Un-fucking-believable," she said and hung up.

July 7

The memorial service for Bill Guest was heavily attended by people from the *Public Sentinel* newsroom. Martin Grimsley, the *Public Sentinel*'s editor, gave the eulogy, and several colleagues rose to share affectionate anecdotes about the dead newsman. Ennis didn't because he didn't think he could hold it together.

Among those in attendance was sports columnist Dietrich. After the service, he approached Guest's sister and said: "I'm sorry for your loss. He was a good man, and we'll miss him."

July 12

Ennis and Penelope were married on this day, a Saturday, just a week after he proposed. It was a small wedding that included their immediate families plus Penelope's co-worker Rhonda Mitchell, who served as bridesmaid, and Saul Lansky, who acted as best man.

Penelope wore a simple, elegant white cocktail dress. Ennis thought she had never looked so lovely. The Episcopal priest was charming in a practiced way. (Sample jokes: "We've had so many shotgun weddings here we call it Winchester Cathedral." And, "I was a Catholic priest until I flunked celibacy.")

After the ceremony, the wedding party adjourned to the Bellevue Stratford Hotel's Hunt Room for an early dinner. In the shadow of city hall, the Hunt Room was infested with politicians during the week, but not so much on a weekend.

Following dinner, the newlyweds drove to a hotel in Beach Haven, New Jersey, for a four-day honeymoon. Ennis exercised enough in the ocean and bedroom to lose four pounds. Penelope asked him if his private parts were weary enough to seek sexual asylum in another country. He explained that he had always expected complete loyalty and dedication from his reproductive organs and had never been disappointed.

July 16

Ennis walked out of Ralph & Rickey's, a restaurant at Tasker and Taney in the Grays Ferry neighborhood. He was carrying one of the Sciulla brothers' culinary *objets d'art*, a Philadelphia cheesesteak with pizza sauce—aka a pizza steak.

Two boys, about 15, were out on the sidewalk near the entrance, punching each other. A patrolman strolled up to the fight scene but did nothing to stop it. He just stood there, scribbling in a notebook and smirking.

The boys seemed evenly matched at first. But now, the taller, redheaded kid was beginning to prevail. His adversary dropped to his knees, bleeding from his nose and mouth, while the redhead continued to punch him in the face.

Angered by the cop's inaction, Ennis put the paper bag holding his sandwich on the sidewalk and strode up to him. "Aren't you going to stop this?" he yelled. "He could kill that kid!"

"Move along, this is police business," the cop said.

"And what business would that be, watching this kid get beaten to a pulp?" Ennis asked.

He then turned and shoved the redhead away from the helpless, bleeding boy, sending him sprawling. He started to help the injured boy to his feet when the policeman came up behind him and yanked him backward. Ennis landed on his ass.

"You boys get the hell out of here before I run you in," the cop said. Turning to Ennis, he added: "And you are under arrest."

"For what?" a startled Ennis asked.

"For interfering in police business," the cop replied. "Now turn around."

The patrolman then handcuffed Ennis and called for transportation to the district police station. Inside the station door, Ennis was promptly recognized by the desk sergeant, Woody Helms, whom Ennis had gotten to know during his year as a police reporter.

Helms saw the handcuffs, pulled Patrolman Martin Fegley aside, and asked him what was going on.

"I'm arresting him for interfering with police business, for disorderly conduct," the patrolman said. "Two kids were fighting and before I could break it up he comes up and tells me in a smart-ass way to stop them. I told him to move along. Instead, he shoves one of the kids so hard he lands on the ground."

Helms walked over to Ennis. "What's your version?" he asked. He was told how the cop just stood there while the bigger kid kept beating the other boy after he had dropped to his knees, bleeding, and that he had pushed the bigger boy away before he could cause even more injury.

"George, have a seat here while I have a word with the patrolman." He then ushered Fegley to the other side of the room.

"This is a bullshit collar, Fegley," Sgt. Helms said. "And to make matters worse, the guy you want to arrest is a reporter for the *Public Sentinel*. If our publicity-minded commissioner learns of this, your career will—shall we say—be put on hold. So I suggest, if you don't want to spend the rest of your career directing traffic in Roxborough, that you go over there to Mr. Ennis, tell him you won't be charging him, and apologize for the misunderstanding."

July 17

City Council had held day-long hearings on Philadelphia's grinding gang problem. Ennis had been pulled off night rewrite to cover them because the editors didn't want Bureau Chief Sumner making one of his murky messes out of a potentially good story. (He was told to concentrate on the Planning Commission meeting.)

Ennis and reporters from the other city papers gathered around Council President Mario Pisano as he left the hearing. Pisano had just started to answer the first question when Channel 13's Lamont Marshall barged through the ring of newspaper reporters with a cameraman in tow—and an interrupting request:

"Pardon me, Mr. President, could you give us a quick moment so we can get this on the air?"

Pisano turned back to the newspaper reporters. "Fellas, let me take a moment to give Mr. Marshall what he needs, then we can finish up."

This touched a nerve. Newspaper reporters were well aware that while they were essentially anonymous, their televised counterparts were not. This subtextual jealousy enhanced their resentment when they felt TV news people were getting preferential treatment from newsmakers anxious to see themselves on the tube.

And so, they got pissed off when Marshall, the arrogant rotten apple in local TV's basket, tried to gyp in at the head of the line. Particularly annoyed was the mercurial Franny Ferrone, a city hall reporter for the *Bulletin*.

Ferrone made his way behind Pisano. When the council president started to answer Marshall's first question, Ferrone stepped even closer to the microphone and began chanting: "Piss, shit, fuck, piss, shit, fuck, piss, shit, fuck . . ."

His print buddies grinned broadly.

Ennis went home that evening to his one-bedroom, where he and Penelope were now living. She greeted him with a smile, a kiss, a drink, and then, with a whiff of pride, served Mrs. Paul's fish sticks, Betty Crocker potatoes au gratin, Birds Eye succotash, and, for dessert, Breyer's strawberry ice cream. Ennis told her the meal was delicious. They finished eating and then settled on the sofa in front of the television. Penelope ran a finger down the bridge of Ennis's nose.

"You're so pretty," she said. "I guess I'll have to spend the rest of my married life fending off other women."

Ennis kissed her hand. "Why would I go out to pick dandelions when I have a rare orchid at home?" he asked.

"Oh, George. I love it when you speak Botanical."

July 18

Ennis had been detached from night rewrite to do a piece for the *Public Sentinel Sunday Magazine*. The idea was to spend Friday, Saturday, and Sunday nights driving around the North Philadelphia ghetto in a patrol car and then report on what happened. He would go on patrol during the 4:00-midnight shift with Sgt. Ralph Spender, a 19-year veteran of the force who referred to less than law-abiding North Philadelphians as "bugs."

They had only been on patrol for 15 minutes when the metallic voice on the police radio announced gang action at 20th and Ontario. Spender hit the siren and the gas and they headed for the intersection.

Ennis could hear sporadic gunfire as they approached the corner. He reflexively got lower in the seat. Spender smiled.

"You planning to have sex with the floor mat?" he asked.

There was another gun report as they closed on the intersection. Scores of gang members were fleeing north on 20th. Spender headed for the center of the intersection and nailed the brakes. The squad car came to an abrupt halt and instantly became a steel island in this fast-running river of boys.

Spender grabbed his billy club, jumped out, and waded against the current of kids, looking for the ones with the guns. Ennis would later marvel at the policeman's guts. But at the moment, he was too busy deciding that he didn't have big enough balls to leave the car and check out the scene. Instead, he scrunched further down in his seat as the teenage tsunami continued to flow around the car.

This proved quite prescient a few seconds later when a bullet tore through the rear window and had enough velocity left to crack the windshield.

In another 30 seconds, the horde was gone, vanished into a gray, grimy masonry wilderness.

Additional patrol cars were arriving. Spender came back to the car and got behind the wheel.

"You okay?" he asked.

"Except for the fact that my balls shrank."

Spender grinned. "I didn't see any shooters," he said. "Guess we'll have to go back to the station and get a new set of wheels. You stickin' with me?"

"Yeah."

They spent the early evening uneventfully, patrolling neighborhoods. As they walked back to the patrol car after checking the doors of several businesses that had closed for the day, Ennis noticed a young man across the street, making his way down the sidewalk in a wheelchair.

"I've seen several guys in their teens and 20s in wheelchairs," Ennis said. What's the story?"

"As you know, these gangs shoot at each other," Spender replied. "You get hit in the spine and you get paralyzed."

Later that evening, after night had fallen, they got a call on a break-in in progress. They started down the half street on which the crime had been reported only to encounter an impassable mound of debris featuring a mattress and a refrigerator. They had to back up, go around the block, and then come in on the other side of the Himalayan trash pile. By the time they got to the scene, the burglar had fled.

An hour later, they stopped in front of a large, once-grand church, one of many abandoned by fleeing whites and taken over by black congregations hard-pressed to maintain them.

"The pastor asked us to check on the church," Spender explained, as they headed up the broad granite steps toward the front door. On each side of the entrance, behind the church's imposing Grecian pillars, were dark spaces where homeless people often slept and copulated.

Spender turned on his flashlight and pointed it in the direction of the grunting. The beam revealed a fortyish man on top of a middle-aged woman without upper front teeth. Spender knew the man.

"Benny, you know you're not supposed to be here," he said gently. "You're going to have to continue your courtship elsewhere."

"Okay, Sergeant," Benny said. "You the man."

Spender studied the pair. "When's the last time you ate, Benny?"

"We had lunch at St. Christopher's soup kitchen. That was it for today."

"Get yourselves a hamburger," Spender said, handing Benny a buck (worth $7.05 now).

Near the end of the shift, they got a radio call saying neighbors were worried about an 81-year-old man living in a rooming house near 22nd and Allegheny.

"No one's seen Teddy in days, and he always goes out for a walk, sure as the sun rises," the landlord told Spender.

The owner used his master key to open the door to Teddy's hot, squalid, second-floor room. Spender smelled the reason no one had seen the old man.

"We'll take it from here," he told the owner.

The old man was sitting at a small, battered kitchen table with his face in a bowl of cereal. Spender closed his eyes, and then let the sadness in them wash over Ennis.

"You know, this business toughens your hide, but you never really get used to this kind of shit," he said, motioning toward the dead man. "I mean, what kind of a way is that to go, alone in a dump like this with your face in a bowl of fuckin' Cheerios?"

Ennis marveled at how this policeman was able to conduct all these vocational expeditions through a big city's cruelest and most leprous landscapes and not let the inevitable carcinoma metastasize—and kill his humanity one cell at a time. He also remembered that cop at Taney and Tasker doing nothing to stop that kid from beating the blood out of that helpless boy—a reminder that not all policemen had halted the spread of the disease.

CHAPPAQUIDDICK ISLAND, MA
July 19

Mary Jo Kopechne, a former Kennedy campaign aide, died in the early morning hours in a submerged car after it was driven off a bridge by Edward M. Kennedy en route from a party on the island.

THE MOON
July 20

Astronauts Neil A. Armstrong and Edwin E. Aldrin, Jr., take man's first lunar stroll.

PHILADELPHIA, PA
July 21

"His motives were certainly delitescent," Ennis said of the embezzler he was writing about.

"Delitescent?" Lansky responded.

"Yeah, it means 'hidden,' 'concealed,' 'latent.'"

"George, you just used that word because you figured I didn't know what it meant."

Ennis put his hand on his friend's shoulder. "Saul, you'll just have to master the meanings of words containing more than one syllable. If you persist in your devotion to monosyllabism, it will have a delusterant effect on our discourse, and I'll never be able to ask you how you feel about antidisestablishmentarianism."

"George, permit me to respond in monosyllables: Fuck a duck!"

July 22

Ennis and Penelope had stopped at the Quill & Scroll for a nightcap after an early dinner at the Sansom Street Oyster House. They joined Lansky at the bar, and Penelope promptly excused herself to call her ailing mother from the club's public phone.

A silent Ennis poured some Rolling Rock and watched its frothy landing at the bottom of the glass resolve itself into beer and head.

"You seem a bit distracted," Lansky said.

"I find my life a bit distracting at the moment," Ennis replied. "I don't think I've done much of a job of managing it so far, and I don't just mean fucking up here and there. I'm really talking about the rudderless nature of my journey to date.

"Some peoples' vocational voyages seem so assured and linear. They've plotted a course toward a destination and maintained their heading. I haven't done that. I don't so much act on history as react to it. I sometimes feel like a leaf carried along on a strong current, washing up, from time to time, on some adventurous rock, then slipping back into the water."

Lansky looked at Ennis quizzically. He wasn't usually so philosophical, at least not this early in the evening.

"I don't know, maybe there is a destination out there for me," Ennis continued. "I'm just not sure what and where it is. All I know is that for me, so far, the adventures along the way have been the thing. For me, getting stories can be adventures, experiential places I've never been. So, while I'd like the idea of a destination sighting on one hand, I fear that that landfall would be at the expense of my travels—and just as boring as Ithaca was.

"You know, the more I think about it, the more I think that finding my destination has to do with getting ahead in a conventional sense, something that doesn't really interest me."

Lansky put down his vodka and tonic. "Come on, George. Let's not hide behind your maritime metaphors. You're as competitive as everybody else in this business. You want to get ahead, you want to be successful."

"Getting ahead in our game usually means giving up writing so you can tell other people what to write," Ennis replied. "I signed on to tell stories, and that hasn't changed."

Ennis took a sip from his glass and then said: "I guess for me, success sounds more like being an able-bodied seaman than an order-barking midshipman."

"So, you do want to be successful," Lansky concluded. "You just want to be a success as a writer rather than as an editor. And by the way, George, I think you're being a bit dismissive when it comes to editors. Good story ideas and sharp editing pencils are precious things."

"You're right, Saul, and I do respect people who have those gifts. It's just that I don't want to stay back on the bridge taking the long view. I want to go ashore."

That night, in bed, Penelope kissed his cheek, then looked at him the way women do when they want answers.

"You and Saul seemed locked in such serious discussion when I came back from the phone."

"It was just one of those beery frat boy conversations about the meaning of life, and I'm not really interested in re-hashing something that would leave you catatonic. Rather, I'm of a turn of mind both Ionic and epic. I want to introduce one of the Sirens to Polyphemus, the one-eyed giant."

Penelope smiled. "Well, I don't know how gigantic he is, but I do love it when you speak Homeric."

Ennis grinned, got out of bed, and walked to the record player by the bureau. He dropped the needle on a new Bobby Dylan song:

"Lay, lady, lay, lay across my big brass bed/Stay, lady, stay, stay with your man awhile/Until the break of day, let me see you make him smile/His clothes are dirty but his hands are clean/And you're the best thing that he's ever seen . . ."

July 25

Ennis parked near the Police Athletic League gym, which was located in a former hardware store on a gritty South Philadelphia street corner. His North Philadelphia patrol with Sgt. Spender the previous weekend had produced a piece the editors liked, so he had been detached again to do a feature on PAL's impact on often disadvantaged boys. He was at this PAL gym to interview two volunteers—Patrolmen Dario Tucci, 28, and Kenneth Snyder, 30. The writer found them at ringside, each coaching one of two welterweights duking it out on a gray canvas surface where previous combatants had marked their territory with blood.

"Keep your left hand up, Marcus," Tucci yelled to his fighter. "You're leaving the barn door open."

"Move to your right, move to your right," Snyder urged Marcus's opponent. "You want to stay away from that right of his."

The helmeted boys traded punches for two more minutes before being sent to the showers.

The two policemen walked over to where Ennis was watching, shook hands, and began answering his questions.

"We come in around three, when school leaves out, work with them a couple hours, then pick up our car for the 4:00 to 12:00 shift in progress," Tucci said.

"What do you feel you are accomplishing with this work?" Ennis asked Snyder.

"Obviously, we are keeping them off the streets, for openers. And hitting someone with heavily padded gloves is a better way to work out your aggression than shooting or cutting them. I think, too, that honing their boxing skills builds their self-confidence. And for some of them, I feel Dario and I are father figures they wouldn't have otherwise."

Ennis spent an hour talking to them and several of the boys then left. Tucci and Snyder climbed into Snyder's 1967 Ford F-150 pickup and headed for the district station where they would get their patrol car. Tucci looked over at Snyder and burst out laughing.

"Kenny," he said finally, "you are so full of shit!"

"You accuse me of harboring excessive poo-poo? I'm stunned."

"I particularly liked learning I was a father figure to those poor boys," Tucci said.

Snyder smiled. "I was going to add that we felt we were giving back to the community by volunteering there," Snyder responded, "but I thought that might be a little too much."

"You are a piece of work, Ken."

Snyder responded: "Look at it this way, my man: We get a double-dip out of this. We get our usual brownie points for volunteering at the gym, plus we'll make the commissioner's dick hard when he reads those 'caring cop' quotes in Mr. Ennis's story."

Four hours later, at 9:15 p.m., Snyder told Tucci to slow down as they neared a dilapidated North Philadelphia two-story. The first-floor storefront was dark, but light seeped from around the blinds of a second-story window.

"Check out the old store's second floor," Snyder said.

"Why?" Tucci wondered.

"My snitch says this is Big Lenny's wholesale drug distribution center. If you want to push horse or blow in this part of the world, you knock on the back door of this shit hole and pay to play. By this time of day, there should be a shit load of dough and dope up there. Anyway, keep moving."

"Why'd you show me Big Lenny's nose candy store?" Tucci asked.

"Because you and I are going to hit it."

"Are you out of your fucking mind?"

"No, I'm not. Hear me out, now. My snitch used to work in the room upstairs. He says the place is usually manned by three people, including the guy at the top of the stairs who watches the surveillance camera aimed at the back door. All of them are armed with .45 automatics. One of them, the guy who watches the camera, also has a 12-gauge shotgun.

"Obviously, we wouldn't try to barge in on that kind of firepower. We'd wait until 11:00 pm. when they close up shop and come out that back door with the proceeds and the unsold dope. We jump them there, put them all in the trunk of their big Lincoln, and live happily ever after."

"I guess it could work," Tucci conceded. "What would it pay?"

"The snitch says that by 11 o'clock Friday night, there's usually about 20 to 30 large in the till. We give our informant five and split the rest. We also get paid when we fence the dope, but I think it would be too risky to do that right away. We'll wait awhile. If we don't, it would just give Lenny a better chance to find out who we are."

"Do you think he'd come after cops?" Tucci asked.

Snyder smiled. "Nobody steals from Big Lenny," he said quietly. "So, anyway, this is a good payday. Are you in?"

Tucci grimaced. "I'd like to be" he replied, "but I just don't have big enough stones to do this."

"Okay. I can't say I'm surprised. Guess I'll have to find another partner in crime."

"I'm sorry, Kenny."

The two recently divorced policemen dropped off their squad car shortly before the midnight close of their shift and climbed in the pickup. First stop was Jimmy's Bar & Grille. The owner, James Cassidy, had six slot machines and a 93-octane poker game keeping the beer kegs company in the basement. His was one of four illicit city businesses that paid $50 a month to Tucci and Snyder's extortion subsidiary.

After several drafts, Tucci said: "Let's get a six-pack and go over to Nancy's place. I'm kind of horny."

Nancy Barnes, 27, was a heroin-addicted prostitute the partners would press into service from time to time. They usually gave her a couple bags of the horse they had pocketed from pusher busts.

July 28

Ennis called Penelope from his desk. When she answered, he said, "I love you" and then hung up.

"Oh, that was so sweet," Lansky said. "You're so romantic. I bet you're a wonderful helpmate, too. Do you dry the dishes and scrub the toilet bowl?"

"Lansky, if you could write half as well as you eavesdrop, your work would have this paper's book critic coming down both legs."

"Ennis, all I can say is that anyone as head-over-heels as you is most certainly pussy-whipped."

Ennis chuckled. "Lansky, may the bird-of-paradise defecate on your new Brooks Brothers sport jacket. But before it does, you better prepare yourself for some notes on deadline from Marvelous Martha Lindner. She's covering the PGW (Philadelphia Gas Works) hearings. Seth would have hung it on me, but I convinced him I was still up to my ears with the pier fire."

"Ennis, if this sort of vile scheming is typical of you Christ critters, no wonder Caligula thought of Christians as high-protein lion snacks."

"Actually, there's no real evidence that the Romans ever fed any Christians to the lions," Ennis said. "On a less nutritious note, how are you finding life at Father Donovan's Home for Wayward Boys?"

"Good," Lansky responded.

"Wish I could say the same about my building. It's just loaded with assholes. I think it was built on an ancient asshole burial ground."

July 29

Arabis hung up his faded denim vest and walked to an open spot at the Quill & Scroll's bar. He was wearing a bright yellow t-shirt that announced in black letters: "No muff too tough/We dive at five."

Cedric the bartender frowned. "Could you put your vest back on?" he asked. "We have ladies in here."

"The hell with 'em."

Jeremy Robbins appeared alongside the 5-8, 145-pound Arabis. Robbins was vice president of the club. He was also 6-4 and 245 pounds, making him bigger than most NFL linebackers of the era.

"Cedric, this man won't be having a drink until he puts his vest back on," Robbins announced. "As a matter of fact, he won't even be here if he doesn't."

"You can't do this to me. I'm a member."

"This discussion is over, dick wad," Robbins said. "Either put on the vest or take a hike. If you do neither of the above, I'm going to throw you down the fuckin' stairs!"

Arabis could sense the adrenaline and testosterone at work in that big body. He put his crummy vest back on.

July 30

Ennis was lying on his back in the wake of their lovemaking. Penelope was staring sleepily and silently at the ceiling, which was her wont after repeated orgasms.

"You, know, it's funny about my feelings for you," Ennis said. "They didn't spring full-grown from a seashell. They sort of germinated from a seed, pushed gradually toward the surface, then erupted into the sunlight.

"Since then, you've become the sun, the heliotropic trigger in my life."

Penelope smiled and kissed the back of his right hand. "Sometimes, you are so sweet I feel like I could die," she said. Then a twinkle elbowed some room in her loving eyes and she added: "You know I love it when you speak Plant Husbandry."

July 31

Janet had an acid flashback 20 minutes after her arrival at the Quill & Scroll. A colleague found her in a fetal position under the sink in the ladies' room.

"Janet," a startled Barbara Gleason cried, "what are you doing under there?"

"I feel safe here."

The fellow reporter, remembering Janet once said that playing the piano soothed her, helped her to her feet saying, "Janet I want you to play the piano for me."

Barbara guided her to the club's piano, sat her down, and asked her to play.

"What's the program? I don't know what to play," Janet said, fearfully.

"How 'bout 'White Christmas?'"

The playing did seem to calm her.

August 1

Menges, the day city editor, placed the phone back in its cradle and turned to a new desk assistant. "Highball's called in hungover, I mean sick," he said to the new hire. "What a surprise. Well, it isn't a surprise, is it, seeing as he calls in sick on the order of once a week? So, assign one of the copy boys to the wire room."

"Why don't you fire his ass?" the freshly minted assistant editor wondered.

"Because the editor of this newspaper told us to give him a job, and because we on the desk don't want to come down on a man who earned the Distinguished Service Cross and a Purple Heart during the Battle of the Bulge."

August 3

Detective Shoustal called Ennis after reading his Sunday piece about PAL.

"George, it's Kerry. How's it going?"

"Great. What's up?"

Shoustal chuckled. "May I give you a little suggestion concerning your work?"

"Sure."

"The next time you do a cop shop feature, you might want to let me know what policemen you've interviewed or plan to interview."

"What prompted that?" Ennis wondered.

"A desire to keep you from celebrating crooked cops. The sergeant you rode with for the North Philly patrol piece is a stand-up guy, a fine policeman. But the two patrolmen you used in the PAL story, Tucci and Snyder, they're dirty. Internal Affairs is sniffin' around their asses even as we speak."

August 4

Highball Harry was sitting in the back seat of his parents' Bentley, being chauffeured to the paper from the family's estate on the Main Line. As the driver came to a stop outside the *Public Sentinel*'s main entrance, another Bentley saloon pulled in and struck the rear of Harry Ralston's aristocratic ride to work.

Highball jumped out and recognized the passenger in the other Bentley as C. Everett Manning, owner and publisher of the *Public Sentinel*. When Manning got out to survey the damage, Highball cleared his throat and addressed the publisher with stentorian authority: "I suggest we let our driver's sort this out, Mr. Manning. You and I have work to do."

Highball then left Manning with a puzzled look on his face and strode into the *Public Sentinel* lobby, where he took the elevator to the newsroom.

"Do you know who that was that just got on the elevator?" Manning asked the man who tended the lobby newsstand.

"Oh, that's Harry Ralston. He works in the *Public Sentinel* newsroom."

"Oh really. What does he do there?" the publisher asked.

"He's the wire room clerk."

"The wire room clerk!" Manning replied, his wide-eyed surprise subsiding into a chuckle. "I thought he was William Randolph Hearst."

August 6

Ennis was sitting in the *Public Sentinel*'s cafeteria at 9:00 p.m., reading the A edition and waiting for Lansky to join him. Both had long stories to finish by the 11:15 deadline for the B. Ennis had started his piece, Lansky had not.

The big guy seemed to have trouble taking advantage of those occasions when he could get an early start on a story. It was as if he had to feel a deadline closing in on him, as if the urgency had to be almost palpable before he could bear down and bang it out. Fortunately, he was Indy 500 fast. (Ennis was not.)

Aaron C. Ledbetter didn't have Lansky's procrastination problem. At any given moment, Ledbetter had 15 to 20 of his semi-weekly columns in the can.

Ledbetter wrote columns on human behavior and relationships which he typically derived from interviews with Philadelphia psychologists and psychiatrists.

His columns were popular with women. Men often found them a bit touchy-feely, which might explain why newsroom operatives not laden with too many jugs of the milk of human kindness called Ledbetter the bedwetter.

Looking up from the Ledbetter column he was reading, Ennis acknowledged Lansky's arrival and allowed that the columnist had a pretty good gig. "I mean, he essentially transcribes a tape recording of his interview with the shrink du jour," he said.

"It's a popular column, George, that's the bottom line. So, you can be damn sure he's making more money than you are."

LOS ANGELES, CA

August 9

Members of the Manson family invaded the home of film director Roman Polanski and his wife, actress Sharon Tate. Fortunately for Polanski, he wasn't home at the time. The Manson disciples killed Tate, who was eight months pregnant, and four others.

August 10

Janet came home from work and had her usual big vodka drink followed by a joint. She still felt a bit down.

"Fuckin' George," she said, barely audibly. Then, thought replaced speech: "Why didn't he fall in love with me? I'm smart and sexy and we're newspaper soul mates. Why would he fall for some fuckin' barmaid?"

She took a last toke from her joint, then a pull right from the vodka bottle. She shivered as it went down unchased, and then dropped some acid.

When the LSD kicked in, she began perceiving ribbons of incredibly fluorescent reds, yellows, and greens. The ribbons of color migrated toward the balcony. She followed them out there, and when they began to float beyond the balcony, she reached out to them. Unsteady from the vodka and the weed, she lurched forward—and fell over the railing.

Two minutes later, a woman walking a dog found Janet's shattered body on the sidewalk 19 floors below her apartment.

August 11

A mountainous Teamster driver was tuning up on shots and beers in Freddie's for his imminent suburban deliveries of the B edition.

"I ought to drop a dime on this guy," Lansky said. "He's going to hurt somebody, or worse."

"You don't want to mess with him," Ennis told Lansky. "He's a reincarnation of Diplodocus."

"Okay, George, I'll play your tedious game: Who or what is Diplodocus?"

"Diplodocus was a huge dinosaur found in western North America late in the Jurassic Epoch. He got to be nearly 90 feet long."

Lansky winced and said: "I shouldn't have asked. It just encourages you to be a jerk. And I know damn well you just came across Diplodocus in the dictionary 20 minutes ago."

BETHEL, NY

August 15

This Friday marked the opening of the Woodstock Festival, those legendary four days in which as many as a half-million young people gathered on a muddy, upstate New York farm for an epic convergence of sex, drugs, and the rock and folk music performed by dozens of artists ranging from Janis Joplin and Joan Baez to Creedence Clearwater Revival, the Jefferson Airplane, the Grateful Dead and Jimi Hendrix.

August 16

Ennis and Lansky attended Janet's funeral, as did most of the newsroom. Afterward, they went to the bar at the Hunt Room. It seemed more in keeping with the occasion than their usual watering holes.

A hunched Ennis looked up from his double vodka tonic. "I should have done something. I should have talked to her about the drinking and the drugs. But I figured she was a grownup and I was in no position to lecture people about booze.

"The last time I talked to her, I told her I had proposed to Penelope. She was really mad. It's hard to say this without seeming incredibly vain, but I'm wondering if that figured in this."

"George, stop beating yourself up. This wasn't your fault. She was a casualty of life. You and I both knew she might well crash and burn."

Ennis wiped the moisture from the corner of his right eye. "Oh,

Saul, it's just such a waste. This wasn't some lady who lunched, some suburban broodmare who contributed to nothing except the census count. She was an excellent writer and reporter. And now, all that talent and skill, all that experience and judgment, have just evaporated.

"This isn't just a loss, Saul. It is incalculable waste."

"A wasteful fate we're all guaranteed the moment we're conceived," Lansky said.

August 18

Patrolmen Tucci and Snyder were sitting in their patrol car, lunching on Big Macs and Cokes.

"Have you found anyone yet to help you boost Big Lenny's ill-gotten gains?" Tucci asked.

"No."

"I've changed my mind," Tucci said. "I've got some big-time markers out there that got to get paid, so I'm in."

"You sure?"

"Yep."

"Well, you might want to change your mind again when you hear the change I've made in our modus operandi. I've decided it's too risky to try to take them prisoner. Too many things could happen. The safest, cleanest way to handle this is to just take 'em by surprise and whack 'em. We'll use our 45s."

"This is nuts!" Tucci nearly yelled. "You're talking about slaughtering three people!"

"These aren't people, Dario, they're Big Lenny's murderous scumbags. We'd be doing society a fuckin' favor by wasting 'em. And we'd certainly be doing ourselves a favor by tying up loose ends.

"So what we got here, Patrolman Tucci, is a big lift for a big payday. You still in?"

"No. I'm out again. I may be a crooked cop, but I'm not a murderer."

"Okay, buddy. Guess I'll have to find another teammate to play slug-a-thug."

August 22

Patrolman Kenneth Snyder had fitted his truck with freshly stolen New Jersey license plates and parked it six blocks from Big Lenny's Drugs 'R' Us facility.

The big smack-and-snow wholesaling operation conducted here every Friday was due to close for the day in an hour, and it was time to get moving.

Snyder hadn't been able to come up with a replacement for his partner, so he decided to go it alone. The idea was to blow away Lenny's crew as they loaded the take and the unsold heroin and cocaine. He would then drive their car to where his truck was parked and transfer the money and drugs.

Snyder hid in an alley near the back door where they would load up. From there, he could sneak up on them and start firing as they placed the boxes and bags of money and drugs in the Lincoln sedan's voluminous trunk.

The trio presently came out the door carrying the drugs and money. One of them put down his load, opened the trunk, and then announced he had to urinate.

As he walked away, the other two started stowing their bags of cash and dope. As they bent to do this, a crouching Snyder came up behind them and shot them both in the back with his silencer-equipped .45.

The third man was zipping up his fly when he heard the reduced but still quite audible gun reports behind him. He spun around and reached for his .45. As he did, a round from Snyder's gun ruptured his Aortic artery, and a second bullet tore open a major vein called the Inferior Vena Cava.

A careful man, Snyder quickly placed another round in the foreheads of his already-dead victims. Then, he tossed the rest of the cash and dope in the Lincoln's trunk and drove away from the still-deserted alley.

After he transferred the loot to his truck, Snyder carefully wiped down the Lincoln for fingerprints.

When he got home, he counted the money and weighed the dope. There was $35,600 in bills. He estimated the street value of the unsold drugs at $20,000.

August 23

It was Saturday morning, but Penelope wasn't sleeping in. At 7:10 a.m. she got up, hurried into the bathroom, and vomited. She came back to bed looking wan and tired.

Could this mean what I think it means?" Ennis asked.

"I have a feeling it does," she replied. "I missed my period and this isn't the first time this has happened. And my breasts are a bit swollen and tender."

"Really? Maybe you ought to see your gynecologist."

"I think I will."

Ennis put his arm around her and kissed the tip of her nose.

"Wouldn't it be great if you were pregnant? Think of the possibilities. If it's a boy, I could teach him how to pick up girls and keep things vague with women."

Penelope bit her lower lip. "George, why is it that when I'm with you terms like 'incorrigible' and 'developmentally arrested' invariably come to mind?"

"Incorrigible? How can such good intentions trigger such a criminal label? I'm talking about mentoring the boy, ameliorating his social skills, and you wound me with a jagged-edged description like that!"

"George, there's a real chance we're having a baby. Can't you be serious about anything?"

"I'm serious about you. I love you so much there are times when I almost can't bear it."

August 26

Leonard J. Reynolds, Jr. stared out the window of his spacious, sixth-floor office, which overlooked a portion of Philadelphia's Fairmount Park. His mind was not on this section of the world's largest urban park, however. It was on, in descending order, the recent theft of valuable assets, and the death of three of his employees.

Everybody called Leonard Reynolds "Big Lenny." There was justification for that. The black 41-year-old North Philadelphia entrepreneur stood six feet, five inches and weighed 390 pounds.

Like Angelo Bruno, the head of the Philadelphia crime family, Big Lenny had a portfolio of legitimate and illegitimate businesses. And like the mob's capo di tutti capi, a.k.a. "the Gentle Don," Big Lenny preferred making money to making enemies and corpses.

Fortunately for Big Lenny, a quirk in Bruno's business philosophy had handed him his most lucrative operation: heroin and cocaine distribution in North Philadelphia. Like the title character in Mario Puzo's 1969 novel, *The Godfather*, the Philadelphia don told his crime family members not to traffic in drugs. But that didn't mean the horse and blow didn't flow in the fiefdom of the man also known as "the Docile Don."

Some of his organization's members, like his consigliere Antonio "Tony Bananas" Caponigro, were dealing drugs behind his back. Others, notably the infamous Sicilian Pizza Connection heroin ring, were permitted to deal in Philadelphia and South Jersey, probably for a piece of the action.

There were also believed to be black ghetto dealers like Big Lenny flourishing during the don's regime, and most of them probably were not tithing at the Bruno basilica. There was apparently no effort on Bruno's part to collect a street tax from the dealers. That came later when Nicky Scarfo took over the mob.

Big Lenny's eyes veered away from the park view and settled on the bound and gagged man on the other side of his desk.

"So nice of you to stop by, Patrolman Snyder," Big Lenny told the wide-eyed policeman. "It's comforting to know you've been checking on our facilities, you tireless crimefighter, you.

"You're probably wondering how we caught up with you so quickly," said Big Lenny, an Ivy League product as well-spoken as he was well-dressed. "It was easy enough. The crew had brought in a fourth man—a kid who just joined the organization—to clean the place after it closed. He was upstairs scrubbing the toilet when he heard the gunfire outside. Shortly after the shooting stopped, he went to a window, and there, loading the Lincoln by the light of that floodlight, was you. He recognized you right away. You were the guy who had busted him a year before for pushing cocaine.

"By the way, that was pretty quick and cold, the way you offed my associates. But enough of your transgressions. Let's get to the business at hand."

Big Lenny removed Snyder's gag and said: "I want my money and my product. Where is it?"

Snyder blinked several times as if to banish the anxiety in his eyes. "I'll tell you where it is, and I'll be your ear at the cop shop," he said. "Just let me walk."

The expression on Big Lenny's face was a fusion of sneer and smile. "We're not negotiating your lease on life, Officer Snyder," he said. "That lease will not be renewed. Nobody steals from Big Lenny, so you are a dead man. What's to be decided here is how you die. There are two options, actually. You can lead us to my stuff and die instantly from a bullet to the back of the head. Or you can fail to tell us, in which case my associate, Lester, will get to play his favorite game. We call it, 'Get the Gonads.'

"Come in here, Lester," he said then. "Show the policeman your game toy."

Lester, a tall, gangly man with a pock-marked face and missing teeth, came through the door carrying a gleaming chrome, pearl-handled straight razor.

"Did you strop that beauty today?" Big Lenny asked.

"Yes, sir."

"Good. Now, Patrolman Snyder—may I call you Kenny?—let me explain how we play Get the Gonads. In phase one, Lester excises your testicles with his surgical steel instrument, leaving you bleeding noticeably as you adapt to your new, rather brief life as a eunuch. We'll do our darndest to keep you conscious so you'll be able to savor phase two. That's when Lester whacks off your dick.

"So which is it going to be, Kenny old bud?"

Snyder leaned forward and puked on his thighs and Big Lenny's silk oriental rug. He then spit out the residual vomit, squared his shoulders, and turned to Big Lenny. The terror in his eyes had diminished. "If you're going to kill me either way," he said finally, "what's the point in giving your shit back? Granted, getting your junk cut off is certainly a slower and more horrible way to die than getting your brains blown out, but dead is dead. And from your standpoint, this will be beaucoup bucks down the crapper 'cause you'll never find your shit."

"True," Big Lenny conceded. "But for me, that would be a cost of doing business. I can't let people think they can steal from me and live."

"You know, killing a cop would also be a cost of doing business," Snyder countered. "In fact, it could cost you your business—and maybe more."

"Tut, tut, friend Kenny. Trying to prosecute a murder case without a body or witnesses is a fairly heavy lift. Thus, you will be cremated and your ashes scattered to the four winds. Rather religious, what?"

Both men fell silent. Snyder thought of telling Lenny that someone else was aware of the heist. But since Big Lenny would figure out who that "someone" was, and since he was going to die anyway, what was the point in getting his partner wasted? So Snyder, for once the few times in his life, waxed altruistic—and said nothing.

"Okay, Lester," Lenny said, "I'm not going to fuck around with this guy anymore. If the prospect of getting his junk sliced off doesn't move him, I don't think long-term torture will, either. So, let's play Get the Gonads."

Three men came into the room and held Snyder down while Lester castrated him. He screamed, and then writhed and bled for nearly ten minutes before Lester stepped in for the phase two cut.

Snyder was still alive five minutes later. Big Lenny fidgeted. "I have an appointment, Lester," he said. "Let's open a couple carotids."

Lester nodded and slashed Snyder's throat with his razor.

August 27

It was 3:30 p.m. Ennis, who had this Wednesday off, was reading the *Public Sentinel*'s previous Sunday magazine when Penelope returned from the gynecologist's office. She was beaming.

"The rabbit died," she said. "Well, it would have died if they still used rabbits for that purpose."

"Oh, Penelope, this is so wonderful. You're so wonderful. I'm so happy."

Ennis hugged her, then kissed her.

"Do you feel well enough to go out for a celebratory dinner?"

"I feel fine."

"I can let you out in front of the restaurant, in case I have to park some distance away."

"George, I'm quite capable of walking. I'm only five weeks pregnant."

August 28

Dario Tucci slowly rose from bed and walked to the bathroom, feeling like ambulatory roadkill, and not looking much better. This had been another largely sleepless night in the wake of Kenny Snyder's disappearance. He had last seen Snyder when the two parted company at the end of their 4:00 p.m. to midnight shift three days earlier. That was the last time anyone saw him.

Tucci had been upset when he learned of the triple killing at Big

Lenny's drug operation. He had asked Snyder if he were part of it and got a seemingly sincere denial. But now, with his partner's disappearance, his suspicion was moving toward conviction: Kenny did run this game—and he was found out.

He thought of going to a superior with Snyder's proposal to hit Big Lenny's place but reasoned that would probably result in nothing other than possibly making himself a target. So, he did nothing other than up his sleeping pill consumption.

August 29

Ennis and Lansky walked into the Quill & Scroll shortly after their shift ended. It was 10:25, and Dunphy was tuned up on double shots and loudly cursing the Protestants in Northern Ireland. He was reaching his potentially pugnacious point, and Ennis didn't want to be within range should he start swinging. So they took seats five stools away.

"So how long is Penelope going to be in Boston?" Lansky asked.

"Until her mother recovers enough from the operation. I'm guessing a week. Speaking of wives, any chance of you and Ruth getting back together?".

"I don't think so. There's just nothing left except the enmity. I suppose it could be worse. There are no kids involved and her nursing job at Jeff (Jefferson Hospital) pays enough to discourage alimony. But while the divorce could be a pretty clean and simple break, I doubt that it will be."

"Are they ever?" Ennis said. "You hear about amicable divorces, but I never knew anybody who had one."

Lansky put down his vodka and tonic and turned to Ennis. "I suspect tonight will be one of the few times you leave the club without a female chaperone."

Ennis nodded. "Yeah, it's not often I've been here not looking to get laid."

"You're an inspirational figure, George, that's for sure."

"Not really. I just got pole-axed by a woman."

"Speaking of getting woman-whacked, I've contracted a milder case of that affliction," Lansky said. "I've been sleeping with Cynthia Jaworski the last couple nights, and that's been a trip. I never dreamed a shy newspaper librarian with horn-rimmed glasses could be such a bedroom terror. She is absolutely insatiable. Honestly, if I keep seeing her, I'm going to need a skin graft on my dick."

"A shy yet insatiable woman wearing horn-rimmed glasses. She sounds like a cliché come true," Ennis concluded.

Up the bar, a *Daily News* city desk editor must have suggested to Dunphy that Northern Ireland Protestants were people, too.

"You're a fucking asshole," Dunphy declared and shoved the *Daily News* desk man into the woman standing next to him.

The desk man was the wrong debate opponent for Dunphy to get physical with. Jeremy Robbins had four inches and 50 pounds on the Irish-American. He also had a compact uppercut that promptly homesteaded on the sports writer's jawbone. Dunphy fell backward and landed on the splintery floor. He was unconscious for nearly a minute before he pulled himself up to a sitting position, shook his head, and spat out blood and a chunk of incisor.

"Looks like somebody finally asked to see Dunphy's cards," Lansky said.

LIBYA
September 1
At the age of 27, Colonel Muammar al-Qaddafi deposed King Idris of Libya. He then established an anti-Western Islamic state ruled by him.

PHILADELPHIA, PA
September 3
With Penelope still in Boston visiting her recovering mother, Ennis suggested that he and Lansky go down to Chinatown for dinner.

"What are you having?" Ennis asked as he unfolded his napkin.

"I thought I'd try a vegetarian dish."

Ennis's eyes widened theatrically. "I never took you for a fad-follower," he said. "You realize that if you persist down this increasingly popular path, you will have to grapple with one of the great questions of our time: Should a vegetarian eat animal crackers?"

"You can laugh, but I've come to believe that vegetarianism might be a healthy way to eat. It's also about reverence for life and being in league with nature."

"Saul, are you jerking off under the table? You know, you and I probably wouldn't even be here if our ancestors didn't use their sharpened stones to kill Bambi and the Easter bunny."

"Trying a meatless entre is not a lifelong commitment," Lansky said.

"Okay," Ennis replied. "I'll have the fried pork dumplings and the spicy beef main dish, and you can order the flambéd fruit fly feces in a truffled mosquito urine reduction."

"Fu-u-u-ck you," a smiling Lansky responded.

September 10

Penelope was in the kitchen, creating the first course: Campbell's tomato soup. A green, frozen, rectangular solid crafted by Birds Eye was busily metamorphosing into boiled spinach on an adjacent burner. The meatloaf she had made from a recipe in the *Public Sentinel* food section was in the oven. A plate held three slices of Wonder Bread she had cut diagonally. Two more plates hosted Tastykake individual peach pies that would be served a la mode. Ennis, who would later compliment her on dinner, was in the Chesterfield chair at the living room end of the living room/dining room, reading *TV Guide*.

"*The Producers* is on TV at 8:00," he announced jubilantly. "Wanna watch it?"

"George, do we have to watch it again?" Penelope asked as she took the meatloaf out of the oven. "You saw that film twice when it was in the theaters, and you watched it twice on TV with me. Isn't that sufficient?

"But Penelope, my child, this is Mel Brooks's masterpiece. It is rich cinematic art. Each viewing reveals insights, nuances and subtleties previously overlooked."

"Oh," Penelope responded. "Well, maybe you're right. The first time I saw the film, I didn't fully grasp the seismic geopolitical import of songs like 'Springtime for Hitler and Germany/Winter for Poland and France.' Clearly, I didn't seize on the significance of some of that song's most profound lyrics, like 'Don't be stupid, be a smarty/Come and join the Nazi Party.' But I see now that those lines were so revelatory, so post-Weimar Republic."

"Twit me if you will, my dear, but you might change your tune when you see how this movie will enrich our sex lives tonight."

"What?"

"I propose a bedroom skit suggested by a moment in the film. You can play the innocent milkmaid, and I'll be the naughty stableboy. On second thought, I'll be the innocent, and you can be a very naughty milkmaid."

"What if I don't feel very naughty?"

"When, since you became great with child, have you not felt naughty?"

"George, you know I love it when you speak Biblical, but I'm not 'great.' I'm less than two months pregnant."

"Well, I think you're pretty great."

Penelope smiled.

September 12

Gretchen Dietrich was finishing her work day at the Bryn Mawr office of Dr. Reginald Sykes, where she was office manager and receptionist. The last patient had left at 4:40 P.M. She and her married employer had finished having sex at 5:05.

The affair was the first step in her evolution, her emancipation. And she liked it. The doctor was more sexually attentive, more gentle than her brother was.

Dietrich was out of town on a story, so she drove to her Center City apartment, changed, and went out to a lively, nearby bar. She brought back a 22-year-old, whose batteries never seemed to discharge.

September 13

Ennis and Lansky finished work at midnight and left by the back door, headed for Freddie's Filling Station a half-block away. Freddie's was a little more expensive than the Quill & Scroll, but it was much handier for a quick, after-work pop. It also had the white-aproned Freddie O'Herlihy, a most substantial shamrock.

Owner/bartender O'Herlihy was a morbidly obese man whose appearance evoked five heart arteries about to hang "closed" signs in their windows. He also had the ability to attach the "roonie" suffix to just about everything he sold. Thus, a steamer of beer became a steameroonie and a double shot was a doubleroonie.

Lansky and Ennis ordered steameroonies and watched a cute young thing give Freddie a parting kiss.

"Freddie," Lansky said, "I get the feeling that ladies are attracted to you, and I'm not sure why. It's not like you closely resemble Paul Newman."

"Well, it is true that I'm a big, fat guy with a teenie-weenie weiner," Freddie said. "But, I do have a nine-pound tongue."

"Well, that is a rather formidable advantage," Ennis said. "I mean, how could a normally tongued man compete with you?"

September 15

"You know, going to the Jersey Shore wasn't really much of a honeymoon," Ennis told Penelope. "So, I've come up with an idea: We will celebrate the three-month anniversary of our wedding by spending a week-and-a-half in a city where neither of us has ever been."

He then handed her a travel agency envelope containing plane tickets to Paris.

Penelope opened the envelope and stared at its contents. "Oh my god! George, this is unbelievable. I've never even been out of the country."

"Neither have I. But I figured we ought to do it now, while we can. It won't be too long before you'll be too pregnant to fly, and then the baby will be here."

PARIS
October 1 to 10

They stayed in Paris's Seventh Arrondissement. Their small hotel was less fashionable than the district, but their tiny balcony did afford a view of the nearby Hôtel des Invalides and its great gilded dome, which sheltered Napoleon's marble tomb.

It was ten days that seemed like a dream sequence in retrospect. Paris was everything Hollywood said it would be. They would walk for hours in the 60ish October air, taking in the sights and visiting the city's ubiquitous tourist magnets. The Louvre, the Eiffel Tower, the Basilique de Sacre-Coeur, Notre Dame, the Arc de Triomphe, Sainte-Chapelle. They experienced them all.

When Penelope began to tire, they would stop at a café. Usually, they would sit at a sidewalk table with their coffee and *pain au chocolat* watching the passersby. Finally, they would take a taxi back to the hotel, where Penelope would have a brief nap before dinner.

Leaving the city behind left them wistful. And although they vowed to return during an as-yet-unborn October, this would be the last time they would see Paris.

FT. DIX, NJ
October 12

It was noon on a warm, clear, breezy Sunday. Temperatures were climbing toward 80, and Ennis was rubbing the greasy sweat on his forehead. Young men and women were pouring out of chartered buses that had brought them from as far as New York and environs to the edge of this Army base 16 miles southeast of Trenton.

The thousands of anti-war protesters ranged from college kids to somewhat older people. Beyond the calculated grunge of their jeans and hair, some of these more senior demonstrators had about them a certain toughness, a veteran veneer beyond their years. Ennis would later tell Lansky that "Some of the women looked like they could take the chrome off your bumper hitch."

The protesters who assembled on the periphery of the base were rather clear about their aversion to the war. A large banner read: "Victory for the Viet Cong/Defeat Imperialism Everywhere."

As the demonstrators began moving across an expansive drill field, headed deeper into the base, khaki-clad soldiers with holstered sidearms double-timed onto the field, where they dropped to one knee facing the demonstrators now some 150 yards away.

The demonstrators started their 1000-foot incursion into the base as an orderly march. But then, they suddenly yelled and charged toward the soldiers. (The onslaught would strike Ennis as an export from antiquity, a horde of Picts and Scots who, having breached Hadrian's Wall, were now on English soil and closing in on the Roman infantry.)

More soldiers, now equipped with gas masks and fixed bayonets, answered with a tear gas barrage that broke the charge.

The tear gas guns created a dense cloud that spread across the field, and Ennis was promptly treated to his first encounter with the chemical. He later told Lansky that he most distinctly remembered the choking and the sense of being shunted into a cerebral siding reserved for thoughts of suffocation.

That night in Penelope's apartment, she and Ennis ate cheesesteaks from Jim's Steaks at Fourth and South and then, without speaking, got up from the distressed little kitchen table and walked the 10 feet to her bed. They stripped and then kissed.

"Why don't you get on top?" Ennis said. "I love it when your breasts bounce."

"George, you do have quite a boob obsession. Didn't your mother breastfeed you?"

"As a matter of fact, she didn't. I was hoping you could provide me with some mammary deprivation therapy. Maybe that remedial treatment would render me less mammocentric."

Afterward, still straddling him, Penelope asked, "So, how was your day at the office, Ozzie?"

"Well, Harriet, you know how the newspaper business is. You have to deal with a lot of gas."

He then told her about the demonstration. She chuckled and his expression grew earnest.

"I love you," he said.

"I love you, too."

Tears formed in her eyes, providing headwaters for the rivulets that subsequently ran down her cheeks.

"I had always hoped you would say that to me, even when I was with Jerry."

"I never said that to any woman before I said it to you."

She wiped her eyes, bent forward, and kissed him. Each of them shipwrecked softly in the peaceful warmth of the other.

October 13

Harrigan put the phone back in its cradle and glanced around at the other men on the city desk. "Harry Ralston has died," he said softly.

"So, Highball has called in dead," said Arabis, who was standing near Harrigan. "I assume his liver will be buried separately with a 21-gun salute."

Harrigan squinted incredulously and said: "You know, your ex-wife was right when she told me you were tasteless and insensitive."

"She meant that in a laudatory way," Arabis replied.

October 14

Penelope was in the kitchen, listening to The Guess Who's new album, *Canned Wheat*, when the song "Undun" came on:

"She's come undun/She didn't know/what she was headed for/And when I found/what she was headed for/It was too late/She's come undun/She found a mountain/that was far too high/And when she found out/She couldn't fly/It was too late/It's too late/She's gone too far/She's lost the sun/She's come undun . . ."

Ennis burst out of the bedroom, rushed to the record player, and shut it off.

Penelope appeared at the kitchen doorway.

"George, I was listening to that."

"I don't want to ever hear that song again!" he said angrily.

Comprehension puckered Penelope's lips.

October 15

Millions took part in a worldwide Vietnam War moratorium. An anti-war speech by Sen. George McGovern drew 100,000. Bill Clinton, then a Rhodes scholar at Oxford, participated in the English version, an act that would become an issue in his subsequent presidential campaign.

October 16

Lansky had come over to Ennis's apartment to watch the fifth game of the World Series. It pitted the American League's hard-hitting Baltimore Orioles against the National League's pitch-rich New York Mets. The Orioles had the "Bird's Big Four" (Boog Powell, 37 home runs; Frank Robinson, 32; Paul Blair, 25, Brooks Robinson, 23). The Mets, who began life in 1962 as a dreadful expansion team, had some kids on the mound with names like Tom Seaver, Jerry Koosman, and Nolan Ryan.

Joe DiMaggio threw out the first pitch for Game 5 in New York's Shea Stadium. (Clara M. Merritt-Ruth, The Babe's second wife, had done this for Game 2.)

Down three games to one in this seven-game series, the stunned Orioles had to win this one to stay alive. And for a while, it looked like they would. The Orioles' slugger Frank Robinson and pitcher Dave McNally touched up Koosman for home runs in the third inning, and by the fifth Baltimore was up, 3-0.

"I knew those guys would come charging back," declared Mets fan Lansky. "They just have too many tools."

"But they left them in the toolbox last game," Ennis noted. "The Big Four were three for 15."

The Mets got right back in it in the next inning, courtesy of the legendary "Shoe Polish Play." The Mets' lead-off hitter, Cleon Jones, looked like he might have been hit by a pitch. When the umpire ruled that he hadn't, Mets manager Gil Hodges stormed out of the dugout, retrieved the ball, and showed it to the umpire. When the official saw the shoe polish smudge on the ball, he reversed the call and awarded Jones first base. Donn Clendenon then hit one over the wall to make it 3-2.

Then, Al Weiss got into the act with something almost as bizarre as the shoe polish drama: A man who had hit just 10 home runs in the previous 10 seasons sent one out of the park to tie the game.

"That's my man Weiss," Lansky said. "We Jews come through in the clutch."

"How do you know he's Jewish?" Ennis wondered.

"Well, with a name like that he could be," Lansky responded.

The Mets tacked on two more runs to win the game and the series. Koosman got his second series win, and the vaunted Big Four went 2 for 15.

"I don't have any celebratory champagne to pour on your head," Lansky said, "so I guess you'll have to settle for Budweiser."

A smiling Penelope appeared in the kitchen doorway and said: "This isn't a frat house, Saul. If I smell beer in that carpet tomorrow, I'm coming after you."

"She's cruel but fair," Ennis explained.

October 17

Dietrich was getting ready for work, which entailed some research in the *Public Sentinel*'s library before going down to the Spectrum to cover the Philadelphia 76ers' season opener against the Los Angeles Lakers.

Finding himself without toothpaste, he went into Gretchen's bathroom in search of some. After a fruitless perusal of her medicine cabinet, he found something of interest in the top drawer of the vanity: a diaphragm and a container of spermicidal jelly.

Dietrich was stunned by the obvious: You don't have to use birth control if you're only having sex with someone who had a vasectomy.

"That fucking slut!" he said loudly. "After all I did for her."

LARAMIE, WY

Also on October 17

Fourteen black athletes were kicked off the University of Wyoming football team for walking into the coach's office wearing black armbands.

BRYN MAWR, PA

October 18

Gretchen Dietrich drove up from Baltimore on this breezy, sunny early fall Saturday, arriving at her brother's Bryn Mawr home shortly after 1:00 p.m. She had had a pleasant visit with her cousin and was looking forward to seeing a play in Center City with a girlfriend.

As she walked in the kitchen door, her brother slapped her face hard enough to send her staggering sideways.

"You filthy pig," he yelled and threw the diaphragm at her. "After all I gave you."

Gretchen felt the initial shock and pain metamorphose into anger.

"Who's the pig?" she demanded. "I was faithful to you until I found lipstick on your collar and underpants!"

Getting angry and standing up to her brother was at variance with the obsequiousness bred by her long-felt fear of the man. That defiance triggered a hard shove. The blow made her fall backward, causing the base of her skull to strike the edge of the Formica kitchen counter as she fell.

The trauma was enough to rupture the aneurysm that had been lurking patiently, like a post-war land mine, near the point of impact. She died shortly after she hit the floor.

Dietrich stood over her with his hands on his hips, breathing heavily. Then, he knelt by her body and probed for a pulse. Finding none, he stood up and looked down once again at the motionless sister he had been sleeping with for the last 14 years.

"Oh, Gretchen," he said aloud, "we had a pleasant enough life. Why did you have to spoil it? Why did you have to be unfaithful to Horst Dietrich?"

He had to figure out what to do with the body. He collapsed into the comfortable confines of his Le Corbusier chair and extracted the cork from his remaining bottle of Chambertin '47. This was, after all, an occasion as special as it was contemplative.

By the time he had finished a glass of this exquisite vintage, he had a plan.

The first step was to place her body on a 9-by-12-foot sheet of black plastic. He then used a pair of pliers from his basement workbench to pull all her teeth. This would make an identification much more difficult in the unlikely event her body was found. He then wrapped her corpse in the plastic and carried it out to the dark driveway, where he deposited it in the trunk of her Ford Fairlane sedan.

October 19
Dietrich got up at seven on this Sunday morning and drove westerly for an hour to French Creek State Park. There, he pulled off the macadam park road near the entrance to an unpaved service lane. He

got a bolt-cutter from the trunk and severed a link in the chain strung across the service road's entrance. After driving inside the entrance, he got out of the car and restored the chain barrier by replacing the missing link with a piece of wire. He then drove the car far enough down the service lane that it couldn't be seen from the public road.

After a quick look around, he took a shovel from the floor of the back seat, walked another 50 yards down the dirt lane, and then turned right into the woods. About 50 yards in, he found a low, wet area where he reasoned the shoveling would be easier, and started digging.

When the grave was about three feet deep, he went back to the car and got his garden wheelbarrow out of the back seat. After making sure no one was around, he lifted the plastic-wrapped corpse out of the trunk, put it in the barrow, and quickly made his way into the forest.

The grave was now partly filled with water. He dumped the body in it and covered it with a layer of rocks before replacing the soggy earth. He then scattered more rocks on top of the grave and finished by covering it with a layer of dead leaves.

Back at the service road entrance, he removed the wire he had repaired the chain with, drove through, then re-installed the wire link.

Finally, he drove to the park's Hopewell Lake, where he walked to the breast of the dam that had created it. No one was close. He underhanded a small black bag into the deep water. It contained a lead sinker—and 32 teeth.

He jettisoned the wheelbarrow and shovel after wiping them for fingerprints, then drove to Center City, parked her car near her apartment, removed the driving gloves he had worn to prevent prints, and walked to Suburban Station, where he caught a train back to the Main Line.

Early that evening, Dietrich called the Bryn Mawr police to report his missing sister. He told the patrolman who came to his home that his sister had left the house Sunday morning, headed for her apartment in Center City. Her plan, he said, was to meet a girlfriend for lunch and then go on with her to a matinee. When Gretchen didn't show up for the lunch date, Dietrich said the concerned girlfriend first phoned her apartment, then called his house. Dietrich said he subsequently drove to Gretchen's apartment and found no one there. At that point, he said he drove home and called the police.

The patrolman told him that, initially, his department would ask the Philadelphia police to look for her car in the neighborhood and ask if it had any new cases involving a woman fitting her description.

PHILADELPHIA, PA
October 20
Philadelphia police found her parked car in Center City, near her apartment. Armed with the spare keys that Dietrich had given the Bryn Mawr patrolman, they searched the car and apartment. The investigation proved fruitless.

October 22
Word of the disappearance of Dietrich's sister had spread through the newsroom. Before entering the sports department, Dietrich had stopped in the men's lavatory long enough to redden his eyes by splashing them with soapy water.

The sports editor, Jim Crowley, came up to him and put his hand on his shoulder. "Horst, we are all praying this will end well," he said, gravely.

"Thank you, Jim," Dietrich replied. "But you know, with each passing day, it gets harder to hope."

"I know, Horst, but we must continue to hope and pray for the best."

Early that evening, Harrigan got a sign-off call from Seymour Kratz, a district reporter assigned to North Philadelphia. Kratz was a longtime *Public Sentinel* hand and a legendary laggard. He worked hard at doing as little as possible and made many creative how-to contributions to the Book of Sloth.

His usual day's end routine included checking the district police blotter after the 4 P.M. shift change, calling in a couple cop shop items, the shorter the better, then heading to his local bar for an hour or so of shots and beers. He would subsequently drive to his Roxborough apartment and then, at his 7 o'clock quitting time, call the city desk to say all was quiet in the district and that he was going home.

"Where are you calling from, Seymour?" Harrigan asked. "Oh, the North Philly train station! You better get out of there, Seymour, because the station is on fire. It's up to three alarms."

October 27

No leads surfaced in the wake of Gretchen's disappearance, and the case grew steadily colder. It looked like Dietrich had committed yet another perfect crime.

On this day, a week after she went missing, Dietrich quietly left the country, headed for Lyon, the culinary capital of France.

After three days of expensive meals graced with superb wines, he boarded a train for Bologna, Italy's counterpart to Lyon. There, he enjoyed still more gastronomical safaris and a social life developed by his hotel's concierge: the company of an $80-a-night call girl ($670 in 2023 dollars) who looked a lot like Gretchen.

October 31

Ennis, on loan to the entertainment department, had walked over to the Philadelphia Repertory Company's theater on South Broad Street to interview its artistic director, Theodore Carden, about the company's new production of Shakespeare's *King Lear*. Carden, who was directing the show that would open in three days, didn't mind entertainment feature writers, which is what Ennis was functioning as. What bothered him were drama critics in general, and the *Public Sentinel*'s in particular.

Midway through the interview, Ennis baited a hook and trolled for a good quote:

"I gather that you don't have too much time for theater critics," Ennis said.

Carden prefaced his response with a small, ironic smile.

"Drama critics are nocturnal creatures," the artistic director explained. "They emerge from their coffins after sunset and drink the blood of theater people. Actors, directors, playwrights, it doesn't matter. They'll feed on anyone who contributes to a show. There are only two ways to stop them: Either brandish a silver cross as they attempt to enter the theater, or drive a stake through their hearts before they can write their reviews."

November 1

Two items caught Ennis's attention as he read this morning's *Inquirer*. Both involved Philadelphia-area servicemen.

1. Army Corporal Terrence C. Connolly, 26, of Levittown, was killed in an aircraft crash in a Vietnam combat zone. A helicopter observer with the First Air Cavalry Division, he had re-enlisted three months earlier after six years of service that included his first tour in Vietnam. He had volunteered to return to the war, his father, William, said, to spare his brother, Pvt. Michael Connolly, assignment to Vietnam.

2. Lance Cpl. Michael J. Rodowicz, of Trainer, an 18-year-old Marine who quit high school because he couldn't wait to join the Corps, died from head wounds suffered in battle.

MEMPHIS, TN

November 3

The Black Monday Protest that took place here was part of a wide-ranging, unifying black reaction to the racism and discrimination they had encountered in this Tennessee city. Several thousand blacks created a line two miles long as they marched through downtown Memphis, seeking goals ranging from a greater voice in school affairs to union representation at a local hospital.

As they marched they chanted: "Go to hell, white folks, go to hell."

November 5

Ennis walked over to Lansky's desk and asked him if he had heard that Sumner, the less than beloved city hall bureau chief, had been mugged in the Broad Street subway.

"He was injured in the attack," Ennis added.

"Nothing trivial, I trust," Lansky responded.

"He got a concussion and two broken ribs."

"That's a relief," a grinning Lansky said. "I was afraid for a moment you were going to say he was treated for minor injuries and released."

"Saul, your schadenfreude is showing."

"I'm not going to ask you what that means because I already know."

"Really?"

"Yeah, it means taking pleasure in someone else's misfortune. For example, Lansky's cup of schadenfreude runneth over when he learned Ennis's colon cancer had metastasized."

November 12

Ennis and Lansky paused in their late evening progress through the newsroom to take in Martha Lindner's new vocational residence. The editors had finally become weary of listening to rewritemen bitch about her feckless reportage and moved her out of city hall and onto the Help Our Neighbors desk, a two-person ombudsman operation that tried to help largely needy people get food and heating oil and solve their problems with merchants and government.

In her new job, Martha had quickly proceeded to disgust her newsroom colleagues by getting on the phone with the people she was supposed to help and loudly bullying and berating them.

She also proved to be the Da Vinci of passive aggression.

Martha's desk abutted that of her co-worker, Audrey Sanders, so that the two women faced each other at close range. Audrey was a sweet, retiring little woman. Everyone in the newsroom loved her. Martha sensed she was the perfect target for a passive aggressor.

Martha kept piles of copies of the *Public Sentinel* on her desk. Over weeks and weeks, those piles gradually expanded to cover more and more of Audrey's adjacent desktop until finally there was only about an 18-inch-square desktop space for her to work on.

Ennis peered at Audrey's truncated workspace.

"Saul, give me a hand," he said.

The two men then gathered wastebaskets from nearby desks, filled them with all the newspapers on Audrey and Martha's desktops, and then put them back where they came from so the cleaning crew could collect them.

November 15

At 7:50 a.m., Ennis stepped onto a chartered plane bound from Philadelphia to Washington. The short flight was whisking members of Philadelphia Executives Against the Vietnam War to a major anti-war demonstration. It was, in fact, the largest U.S. anti-war demonstration ever. An estimated 500,000 attended.

Bespoke suits and monogrammed shirts abounded on the plane. Ennis felt a little under-dressed in khakis and a coffee-colored corduroy sport coat from Sears.

He interviewed a couple of businessmen on the flight down and planned to get a reaction to the march on the way back. In the meantime, suddenly it seemed he was part of a cast of thousands on Pennsylvania Avenue, a moving mass restrained enough to rule out mob status, yet imbued with a kind of emotional energy that only causes can spawn. The noisy, dramatic breadth of it all left Ennis feeling very alive and excited.

But years later, Ennis's most vivid memory of the march would be that 20ish wisp of a woman perched on the shoulders of a striding young man. As she passed the White House, she raised a diminutive fist and yelled: "Nixon, pull out like your father should've."

November 28

The informational dam built by Army cover-ups and journalistic ineptitude had essentially kept the atrocity from the public since it occurred on March 16, 1968. But by November 1969, some 18 months later, the dam holding back the story of the My Lai massacre had begun to develop grievous cracks.

Chief among them was a damning piece transmitted on November 13 by a small, independent wire service. Written by a freelance investigative journalist named Seymour Hersh, it was picked up by 30 newspapers and promptly gained legs.

Major media, which had been missing this story, got off their asses after the Hersh piece hit. *Time* published a major report on Nov. 28, followed by a big story in *Life* magazine. Finally, a nation had become fully aware of one of the most horrific atrocities in U.S. military history—and it was outraged.

My Lai wasn't so much a military operation as a descent into madness. About 100 soldiers from the Army's Americal Division were dispatched to this area, thought to be a Vietcong stronghold, and told to kill the resisting guerillas they would find there.

What they found, instead, were unarmed women, children and old men, many of them readying breakfast. The troops proceeded to burn huts, rape women and girls as young as ten, and shoot people. Hundreds were shot, a number of them not yet dead when they were tossed into ditches.

NEAR LIVERMORE, CA

December 6

On this day, on the grounds of the Altamont Speedway, a chronological and symbolic end came to a volcanic decade that married peace and love to war and assassination.

The occasion was a multi-band free concert arranged by the Rolling Stones. The affair drew an estimated 300,000.Security was provided by members of the Hells Angels motorcycle gang, who were compensated with $500 worth of beer.

A photograph shows a Hells Angels member fatally stabbing a gun-wielding black teenager. Other concertgoers were beaten with pool cues by the Hells Angels. In all, four people died at the concert, including the one killed by the Hells Angels member, and three accidentally.

Also on this Saturday, in Chicago, several police cars parked in a precinct lot on Halsted Street were bombed. The Weathermen claimed responsibility, saying this was a protest for the fatal police shooting of Illinois Black Panther leaders Fred Hampton and Mark Clark two days earlier.

PHILADELPHIA, PA
December 8

Ennis pivoted away from his trusty Royal typewriter and answered his phone.

"Mr. Ennis?"

"Yes."

"This is Clarence Reynolds. You remember me. You wrote an obituary last May about my son, Teddy, after he was killed in Vietnam."

"I remember you very well, Mr. Reynolds. Is there something I can help you with?"

"They're callin' my son a baby killer!"

"Mr. Reynolds, your boy wasn't a part of that My Lai search and destroy mission. In fact, he hadn't even arrived in Vietnam when the My Lai massacre took place."

The anger in Reynold's voice rose with its volume: "But these bastard protesters make it sound like every soldier in country was a butcher, and that's not right. I still have the Luger I took off a dead German at Bastogne. I have half a mind to take it to one of these protests and shoot a couple of these draft dodgers where I was shot at Bastogne—in the ass!"

"Mr. Reynolds, that's crazy! It won't accomplish anything other than make you spend time in jail instead of with your family."

"Who says they'll catch me?"

"Listen, why don't I come down to Grays Ferry and we'll talk about this?"

Reynolds was silent for several seconds, then agreed to see Ennis. The reporter used his dinner break to meet the troubled father.

Later, in a bar near Reynolds' row house, the two men sipped Schmidt's drafts while Ennis worked to calm him down. Eventually, he got Reynolds to promise not to attend any of these sure-to-be incendiary demonstrations.

December 31

Ennis was sitting in his living room, listening to Creedence Clearwater Revival. They were partway through "Bad Moon Rising," one of his favorites:

"Don't go around tonight/Well, it's bound to take your life/There's a bad moon on the rise . . . Hope you got your things together/Hope you are quite prepared to die . . ."

1969 EPILOGUE

On February 10, 1970, Penelope Rehnquist-Ennis went into early labor and began bleeding heavily. Ennis drove her to Jefferson Hospital's emergency ward where the physician in charge immediately sent her to surgery.

Doctors worked on her for 75 minutes. At 2:44 p.m., a surgeon named Ross M. Samuels emerged from the operating room. His scrubs were soaked under his arms and his eyes were rife with the "eternal note of sadness" that the poet Matthew Arnold had heard in the surf and pebble friction of Dover Beach.

"Mr. Ennis?"

"Yes."

"I'm so sorry. We couldn't stop the hemorrhaging. We couldn't save your wife or the baby."

The surgeon paused here, wondering if he should say it.

"It was a boy," he said, finally.

PART TWO: 1999

AT SEA IN THE CARIBBEAN

January 1

George Ennis was sitting in a canvas deck chair on the bow of a 110-foot yacht called The Other Woman, which had left Fort Lauderdale bound for Pointe-à-Pitre, the principal city of a French Caribbean archipelago called Guadeloupe. The craft's forward progress created a soft, early evening breeze. Ennis took a sip of 18-year-old single malt whiskey from an etched, hand-blown glass and decided life could be worse.

He was on this two-week cruise as one of seven guests of Charlotte Ronson, an heir to the Sterling Farms frozen food fortune. Charlotte was 63 but looked 53 thanks to some exquisite facial surgery. Her appearance also benefited from exercise and her restraint in selecting the size of her breast implants. Unlike some women, she didn't err on the DD side of C.

Charlotte liked having the 57-year-old Ennis as an escort and travel companion. He was good company and decorative, thanks to a still-handsome face and a body rendered taut and defined by regular weight training. He also made her happy in bed.

But she didn't want a serious relationship with him, certainly not marriage. (The rich tend to marry each other.) Ennis sensed this and didn't mind at all. The occasional social event and boat ride were one thing, a live-in situation was another. He wasn't interested in becoming the world's oldest gigolo—or in giving up the company of the several middle-aged women he also saw.

The thing about plus-60 Charlotte and his forty- and fifty-something companions was that, unlike the women he had dated earlier in his life as a widower, they were no longer interested in reproduction—and this, for Ennis, was a welcome development.

In the hideous aftermath of Penelope's death, Ennis decided that he would never risk history repeating itself. The thought of another dead wife, another dead child, another Saharan encroachment on his soul, was just more than he could bear. And so, three weeks after Penelope's funeral, he had a vasectomy.

When he started dating, 18 months later, Ennis soon found that the sterilization had a fringe benefit: If a relationship lasted long enough that the woman would start talking about propagation, he would play the "V" card. Mentioning the vasectomy typically triggered this sort of conversational chain reaction:

Q. Can the operation be reversed?

A. That's rather unlikely at this juncture.

Q. Would you consider artificial insemination or adoption?

A. No.

Q. Why not?

A. Because I don't want someone else's child.

Sometimes, the woman would end the relationship on that note. If she didn't, he eventually would.

Ennis had dozed off after finishing his single malt. Charlotte came up behind him and stroked his gray-streaked mane.

"Dinner is served, handsome."

"Just handsome? What about charming and charismatic?"

"Those, too."

Also on this New Year's day, The U.S. finally ceded the Panama Canal it built to the country that waterway bisected. There had been some objection to the hand-off when it was debated 20 years earlier. Among the protesters was S.I. Hayakawa, who had worked as an author, professor, and university president before becoming a U.S. senator from California. Quoth Sen. Hayakawa: "We should keep the Panama Canal. After all, we stole it fair and square."

January 19

Ennis took a sip of his vodka and tonic and peered out the window of his 8th-floor condominium overlooking Washington Square. A young woman was emerging from beneath the trees, walking south toward Ennis's building.

Her hair color and stride reminded him of Penelope, but then that was hardly unusual. Young women often evoked her, and the conjuring, in turn, disinterred the bones of their life together. In this case, it was Penelope in Paris standing on the sidewalk halfway across the Pont Neuf. She had been looking out over the Seine as it made its gray way past the old bridge beneath her, holding the bouquet Ennis had just bought from an old woman on the Rive Gauche. Then, she turned toward Ennis so that he could snap her picture. Her pregnancy was still virtually imperceptible, and her slight smile struck Ennis as something shared with the Mona Lisa. Now, as then, he was thinking that this scene did not need to be immortalized on film.

Then his thoughts turned to this: "The one woman I loved is dead and, in an unspeakably perverse way, her death has set me free. I'm just haunted by a line from 'Me and Bobby McGee': 'Freedom's just another word for nothin' left to lose.'"

January 24

Seth Menges had called Ennis to tell him that his retired editor, Denny Harrigan, had suffered a massive stroke. Ennis phoned Lansky, and the two went over to the Hospital of the University of Pennsylvania to see him.

Harrigan was unconscious, on life support. Family members stood silently in the gloom engendered by the doctor's prophecy. The arrival of the Harrigans' priest compounded the religious feel of it all. A red-eyed Mrs. Harrigan whispered a benediction in Ennis's ear: "He has no brain activity. May God bless him and take him."

January 28

The memorial service for Harrigan was held late Thursday morning. Afterward, Ennis and Lansky, with a heightened sense of their mortality at ages 57 and 61, respectively, walked out onto the sidewalk in front of the church and reflected on Denny.

"Well, he did live to be 75," Lansky said. "I guess that's a testament to the efficacy of modern medications for the hypertensive."

"I really liked Denny," Ennis said, "even though he was always pulling my chain. Remember when he said he was going to assign me the world's worst story when I twitted him about the Mystery Shitter?"

"He pulled mine, too," Lansky added. "I'll never forget when he threatened to make me take every fucking sewer authority story that came down the pike if I didn't pay reparations to that loony Levandowski."

"Ah, yes, Boris," Ennis said. "He's gone, too."

"So's that big copy boy, Martin Jamison," Lansky added. "I often wondered if he was the Mystery Shitter. He certainly disliked Denny enough to leave those turds by his desk, and the doo-doo deliveries did stop after he was found dead in a ditch in South Jersey. Guess we'll never know."

Ennis's eyes were far away and glistening. "Denny had a 'gotcha' sense of humor," he allowed. "In the end, he was a sweet guy with a moral compass. I missed him after he retired. Still do."

That evening, Ennis and Lansky headed down to the Quill & Scroll in Ennis's 1994 Porsche 911 cabriolet. A tape of a 1978 Warren Zevon song was playing.

"I'm hiding in Honduras, I'm a desperate man/Send lawyers, guns and money/The shit has hit the fan . . ."

"George, do you ever listen to any pop music other than golden oldies?"

"Nope. The 60s and 70s, maybe a little 50s, that's where I live. You get locked into your generation's tunes and don't much like what came before and after. And Auden was right: We do become our parents. My dad hated rock and I despise rap."

It was 8 o'clock when they arrived at the Quill & Scroll. At an earlier moment in history, a Friday night would have seen the place teeming with thirsty editors and reporters who would be joined later by the servers and bartenders who used the Q&S as an after-hours club. But now, the hordes of yore had metamorphosed into Ennis, Lansky and the bartender.

When no one in that trio was talking, the silence of the sepulchre prevailed. On the walls, the pen-and-ink visages of Philadelphia newspaper notables paused as they hurried into history to smile down ironically on two one-time residents of their vanished venue.

Ennis let his eyes run down these familiar rows of drawings, permitting his art museum variation on speed reading to evoke another life, another time—a time when Penelope was still so wonderfully alive.

"Just seems like yesterday that this place was so noisy and alive, so full of smoke and bullshit," he said. "Now it's a cemetery haunted by the ghosts of our dead friends and our dead youth. Hell, even the beer taps seem like grave markers.

"Things are so different now, I guess because the people in our business are so different. We lived in the city and drank and fucked a lot. These people don't drink much and they don't live here. They escape to the suburbs when the 5 o'clock whistle blows, then run around the block and drink a glass of carrot juice. I mean, they seem so yuppie-duppie, so corporate. Where's the soul here?"

"C'mon, George, those kinds of generalizations are always unfair. And just because they live cleaner and smarter than those of us with hob-nailed boots for livers doesn't mean they are devoid of soul. And it certainly doesn't mean they aren't good newspaper hands. Fact is, this newsroom generation is a lot better than ours was."

"Probably true," Ennis responded. "It's also true that this editor had more to spend on talent than old Grimsley did.

"But fuck that. Yes, the *Public Sentinel* newsroom of our youth may have been a less talented place, but it was a more visceral and romantic one. And we had more fun."

January 29
Ennis was sitting in the paper's cafeteria, reading the account of the benefit concert the night before for Mumia Abu-Jamal, a Philadelphia radio journalist and former Black Panther sentenced to death following his conviction for the 1981 killing of Daniel Faulkner, a white, 26-year-old city policeman, after Faulkner stopped Abu-Jamal's brother for a traffic violation.

Abu-Jamal didn't testify at his 1982 trial, and, in the ensuing 17 years, never denied murdering Faulkner. But in books and radio broadcasts from prison, he proclaimed that he had been railroaded by an unfair justice system and became an international cause célèbre, counting Hollywood actors and former French first lady Danielle Mitterand among his supporters.

The concert in a New Jersey arena featured three bands: Chumbawamba, Rage Against the Machine, and Bad Religion. A sign in the arena parking lot read: "Free Mumia. Refuse, Resist."

Ennis looked up as Lansky took a seat at his table and asked: "Did you read this morning's Free Mumia story?"

"Yeah."

"You know what gets me about this guy?" Ennis asked. "Over all these years, he has never once proclaimed his innocence. Yet despite that, people from all over the world keep throwing money at him."

January 31
As the dinner party in the Center City townhouse of Cedric C. Witherspoon III wound down, Ennis and Charlotte adjourned to her nearby pied-à-terre on toney Rittenhouse Square.

(The square was also the Philadelphia home of Henry McIlhenny, who gave a legendary annual gay ball at his castle in Ireland. Relatively late in life, he visited another rich person at that man's home on the posh northern end of New Jersey's Long Beach Island. It was his first time on the island. "It was quite interesting," McIlhenny said later, "You cross the bridge onto the island, and the Haves turn right, and the Have Mores turn left.")

Charlotte's apartment was predominantly contemporary (much chrome and white leather) with an interspersion of antiques, notably large Chinese urns. Ennis saw it as elegant eclecticism.

Charlotte disappeared into the bathroom, where she applied a vaginal cream intended to make intercourse more comfortable.

After their coupling, Ennis rolled off her onto the 800-thread-count sheets. She smiled at the ceiling, then looked over at him and said, "You do know how to make the ladies happy, at least this one."

"You came twice, didn't you?" he said with a smile.

"Which is two orgasms more than men usually trigger," she replied.

February 10

As he did on each anniversary of his wife's death, Ennis traveled 55 miles to a sprawling cemetery near her native Reading, Pa., to place a bouquet at the base of a granite gravestone that read: "Penelope Rehnquist-Ennis 1943—1970."

In the wake of the autumnal equinox, this Southeastern Pennsylvania countryside becomes a gaunt, ghostly place where gray conspires with brown and the only chromatic relief besides the snow is the evergreen, an arboreal minority marginalized by the leafless tyranny of the deciduous majority.

There was a cold, audible wind punctuating this annual reunion's inhospitable environment. That wind picked up, causing even unleafed limbs to shudder. The clouds, gray and infuriated, sidestepped rapidly across the sky.

Ennis shivered, placed the flowers, and produced a silver flask from one overcoat pocket and two shot glasses from the other. He filled one with single malt whiskey and set it atop the gravestone. He then filled the other and raised it.

"Here's to you, kid," he said and drained his glass.

Presently, Ennis returned to his car and fired up the engine and the CD player. An Irish-American band was partway through their cover of "Danny Boy":

"He'll come and find the place where I am lying/And kneel and say an 'Ave' there for me/And I shall feel, though soft you tread above me/And all my grave shall warmer, sweeter be/And you will bend and tell me that you love me/And I shall rest in peace until you come to me."

Ennis shifted gears and brushed his eyes with the cuffs of his overcoat.

February 12

The impeachment proceedings against President Bill Clinton in the wake of the Monica Lewinsky scandal, for perjury and obstruction of justice, were initiated by the House in 1998 and made him only the second U.S. president to be impeached. (The first was Andrew Johnson, 130 years earlier.) He was subsequently acquitted of these charges by the Senate on this date in 1999.

March 20

Ennis's parents were planning to move into an assisted living facility and had put their house in King of Prussia up for sale. That meant he had to get the filing cabinet containing Bill Guest's papers out of their attic. So, he had shown up at their house on this Saturday morning with Saul Lansky's station wagon. (His Porsche 911 didn't have enough cargo space to haul a Mickey D hamburger if you got it with cheese.) He also arrived with a sore back, the result of a 57-year-old man trying to lift the weights he lofted easily at 27.

Normally, he simply would have grabbed the cabinet and carried it out to the car. But because of his bothersome back, he had decided to take the three drawers out and carry them separately. On his third trip, he removed the bottom drawer—something neither he nor the detectives had done in the wake of Guest's death—and noticed a manila envelope on the floor of the cabinet.

Ennis sat down and opened the envelope, saw the first photograph, and gasped. He then leafed through the other nine pictures of Dietrich and his sister having sex on the kitchen counter, and read Guest's research on Dietrich's hit-related travels.

Ennis sat there on that plywood attic floor, inundated by an amalgam of shock and anger. Here was the reason for his friend's murder, as well as the man who killed him, and it had been within his grasp all this time.

He looked around at the dusty dregs of his parents' earlier life and then closed his eyes. "You rotten, murderous bastard," he said quietly. "But I got you now, you cock suckin' fuck. You're meat."

When he got home, he called his old friend Kerry Shoustal. The former Philadelphia detective had retired after 30 years on the force and was now head of security for a Chester County business park. He told Shoustal what he had found and asked to show it to him.

"George, you should be showing this stuff to a detective who's still on the job."

"I'll do that. But first, I wanted to show it to you and get your thoughts on how this thing will probably go down."

"Okay, come on over about 7:00."

Shoustal had moved to a 19th-century farmhouse in Northern Chester County after his retirement from the city police force. Fixing it up had become his hobby. He and Ennis walked across the living room's recently re-finished quarter-sawn, yellow pine floors and took chairs by the native stone fireplace. Shoustal studied the photographs and Guest's findings.

Shoustal handed the materials back to Ennis, removed his reading glasses, and gave his take on what happened: "I think your friend was trying to blackmail Dietrich with this stuff, and Dietrich was able to force him to give up the copies left for you in his safety deposit box. He then broke into Guest's apartment in search of more copies, satisfied himself there were no more, then tied up a loose end when Guest came home."

"I remember telling you I couldn't believe Bill would shake anyone down. I was pretty naïve, wasn't I?" Ennis said.

Shoustal shrugged. "The guy was your friend," he said.

"So, Kerry, where do we go from here?"

"I'll call the head of Homicide tomorrow and tell him what we got, and that you're bringing it in. I'm thinking he'll probably want to question Dietrich and try to get a confession before he lawyers up.

"The more I think about it, the more I think a confession may be the only way we're going to nail this guy. I mean, this is a weak case. No one saw Dietrich in or near Guest's building when he was killed. There is no indisputable evidence that Guest tried to blackmail him. There were no weapons or fingerprints found at the scene. All we have are some photographs and notes found 30 years later 30 miles from the crime scene."

Shoustal paused and then said, "Wait, if Homicide can't get a confession, there is still one small ray of hope: Photos of him sent to the departments in the towns where the hits took place could yield something. But, that's a long shot."

"Kerry, are you telling me this monster might walk?"

"He could very well."

"That's just obscene!" Ennis said. "God knows how many people he's murdered since he butchered Bill. And for all we know, he's still at it. And while we're talking about the activities of this bloody beast, what about the sister he was fucking? She disappeared mysteriously and was never found. Something's gotta be done!"

"You're preaching to the choir, George. I wanted this guy bad when I was on the job, and I still do."

March 22

Gino Infante, the head of the homicide division, ushered Ennis into his office on this Monday morning. Ennis handed him the manila envelope containing the trip research and seven of the 10 Dietrich sex photographs he had found. Infante perused the photos and read Guest's findings.

"That's truly disgusting, banging your sister," he said, shaking his head. "You know, Kerry briefed me on this, and I tend to agree with him: This guy is probably guilty as hell, but this case may well be a dog that won't hunt. We don't have any witnesses, and we don't have any evidence that would put him at the scene or show that Mr. Guest tried to blackmail him with the photos.

"I also agree with Kerry that our best chance is to get him to confess. Otherwise, there'd be no point in charging him. The D.A. would just decline to prosecute. But, who knows, maybe we can pull his chain enough to get him to blurt it out. That's a long shot, given his probable legal smarts, but stranger things have happened.

"If that fails, we'll send out his photo to the other departments like Kerry said, but that's a long shot, too. And If we don't nail him on a murder charge, he's pretty much home free."

"That's great!" Ennis said angrily. "A beast who makes Jack the Ripper seem like St. Francis of Assisi will probably skate. He gets away with murder over and over again, and nothing can be done about it."

"I'm sorry, Mr. Ennis, I really am, but we have to play with the cards we're dealt. And in some cases, we just have to fold."

Ennis left Infante's office, thinking about what he might do if Dietrich walked.

As he drove home, he turned on a golden oldies station where a 1972 Billy Preston song, "Will It Go 'Round in Circles" was in progress: "I've got a story, ain't got no moral/Let the bad guy win every once in a while."

"Fuck the bad guy!" he yelled, slapping the steering wheel.

March 23

Atypically, Infante didn't delegate the interrogation of Horst Dietrich. He went to Dietrich's home in the company of one of his top detectives, intent on questioning him himself.

A knock on the door of Dietrich's expensive Bryn Mawr home produced the sports columnist in a silk robe he had purchased at Dior's flagship store in Paris.

"Mr. Dietrich? My name is Geno Infante, "I'm head of the Philadelphia Police Department's homicide division. This is my colleague, Detective Marshall Brisbane. We have some new information about your sister. May we come in?"

"Yes. Certainly."

Dietrich motioned toward a pair of burgundy aniline leather easy chairs. He took a seat opposite them in his Le Corbusier chair.

"So, what have you learned about my sister?" he asked.

"This," Infante said, rising to hand Dietrich the photographs of him having sex with Gretchen.

"These pictures were found, albeit belatedly, in a filing cabinet that had been in the apartment of a man named William Guest. Mr. Guest was murdered in that apartment 30 years ago by someone who also ransacked the place. We believe that person was looking for these pictures after Guest tried to blackmail him with them."

Detective Brisbane now got involved in what would prove a kind of interrogational tag team match: "Like our detectives 30 years ago, you didn't take the bottom drawer out of his filing cabinet," Brisbane said. "If you had, you would have found the pictures on the cabinet floor."

Predictably stunned, Dietrich initially found it hard to think. He blinked repeatedly, trying to clear his head. But by the time Brisbane had finished, he knew what he would say:

"This is preposterous. You're suggesting I killed that poor man. Look, I admit Gretchen and I got drunk one night and things got out of hand. Obviously, someone was at the kitchen window and photographed us. I don't know who would do such a thing, but I do know that no one tried to shake me down with these pictures. I didn't even know they existed until you showed them to me.

"I'm mortified by them, but I didn't kill anyone because of them."

"Come on, Mr. Dietrich," Infante said. "Mr. Guest didn't take those photos for his scrapbook, and they would have destroyed your career and your reputation."

"And why do you suppose Mr. Guest went to the trouble of doing all that research on your travels?" Brisbane interjected. "That research, which I have here, could have led to something a lot worse than joblessness and disgrace. Photographs of you, circulated to the police departments where these hits took place, may very well have jogged someone's memory."

"You know," Infante said, "there is a less painful way out of this: Confess to Guest's death and you can avoid the minute examination of all the sordid details in open court."

"This is ridiculous, and I'm not going to discuss it anymore without having my attorney present," Dietrich said.

The columnist looked down at his hands after he said this. Brisbane reached in his breast pocket and pulled out a small camera. When Dietrich looked up some five seconds later, Brisbane snapped his picture.

"You can't do that!"

"Of course I can," Brisbane replied.

The two policemen got up to leave. Infante said: "So, you go ahead and lawyer up, Horst. Meanwhile, we're going to be circulating your picture to the police departments where those hits took place.

"Oh, and by the way, we don't know whether our source gave us all of the incest photos. If that person didn't, heaven knows where they might show up."

As they walked to their car, Infante said to Brisbane: "Well, I think we rattled that fucker's cage a little, and that's a start."

After his guests had left, Dietrich went into his study and poured himself a glass of 10-year-old burgundy.

"Whom do these crass imbeciles think they're dealing with?" he asked aloud, as he paced around his home office. "I'm not some corner boy playing softball in the South Philly beer leagues. I'm a major league assassin, a professional. So, if they think they can con me into a confession, that would be a wrong number."

He took a seat in his office chair then and thought about how this thing might shake out. If the photos did see the light of day, he reasoned, he would be fired and disgraced. But at 61 he was in the twilight of his career anyway, and he had the money to live comfortably and anonymously in the south of France. He had enjoyed Aix-en-Provence. And Collioure, the seaside resort where Picasso painted, had proven delightful.

When the two detectives got back to the office, Brisbane had prints of the Dietrich headshot developed. He then sent them, and a description of the case they were trying to make against him, to the police departments in the cities where the murders took place.

March 24

Lansky had come over to Ennis's apartment. After Ennis briefed him on the Dietrich developments, the two sat down at the dining room table and started playing blackjack and drinking beer.

"I've been noticing some things about the aging process," Ennis said.

"You aren't going to tell me a mournful tale about a limp dick are you?" Lansky asked.

Ennis smiled. "No, I was thinking about how I seem to become a more intense sports fan the farther I get from my playing days. When I was younger, I really wasn't that interested in watching football. Now, I never miss an Eagles game.

"I also seem to do more Mittyesque daydreaming. Recently, I've been a 57-year-old guy who becomes a major league sensation when he discovers he can throw a baseball 120 miles an hour for strikes.

"I'm also an incredibly well-built, 6-6, 240-pound high school senior who is brilliant at football and basketball and gets to sleep with his best friend's mother, a lovely widow. And let's not forget the dashing war correspondent and the handsome English field surgeon who returns from the Crimean War and falls in love with a gorgeous London aristocrat.

"You ever do the Walter Mitty thing?"

"I sometimes daydream about sleeping with women who wouldn't dream of sleeping with me," Lansky replied, "but that's about it. And if I did daydream about being a dashing war correspondent or a handsome field surgeon, I sure as hell wouldn't tell you."

Lansky then tapped the stack of cards. "So, ah, does the handsome field surgeon want a hit, or is he sticking?"

"I'm sticking," Ennis replied, looking up from his cards. "And I'm thinking, so much for bearing your soul to an insensitive cad. Who knows what he'll do with the information?"

"Don't worry, George, the secret of your 120-mile-an-hour fastball is safe with me—unless, of course, you fail to buy me a double Stoli after work tomorrow."

April 5

Ennis called Infante and asked if there had been any breaks in the case.

"The police forces we contacted agreed to have someone review the cold case files and show Dietrich's picture to whatever witnesses and neighbors might still be around. Nothing so far."

"It's been two weeks," Ennis said.

"I know, but we'll just have to sit tight for the time being."

April 19

Two more weeks had passed and still nothing from the police departments that Brisbane had contacted. An angry and depressed Ennis visited his friend, retired Detective Shoustal, in his farmhouse.

The two took chairs near the fireplace.

"This investigation is going nowhere, Kerry. Infante and Brisbane have done all they can—and zilch. So, let me put a hypothetical to you: What if there were more fuck-your-sister photographs than the police were given? What if copies of those pictures were to turn up in the desks of *Public Sentinel* writers and editors? Do you suppose that would flush the fucker out?"

"Oh, that would flush him out, alright, hypothetically speaking. And, hypothetically speaking, it would be a good way to get your hypothetical ass shot off. This guy almost certainly remembers you were Guest's good friend and is pretty sure you gave the police the photographs. He probably decided there was no upside to killing you. It would be risky, and pointless in the sense that the police already have the pictures. But if you make it your business to embarrass him and ruin him, he might just get pissed off enough to come after you."

"Good," Ennis answered.

"No, it's not good, George. As you damn well know, this guy is not your garden variety murderer, he's an experienced assassin, a pro. You don't stand a chance against him. If he wants you, you're a dead man."

"I understand how dangerous he is. I know he must have a dozen different poison-tipped arrows in his quiver. But I suspect that he will not want a quick, clean kill from a distance. He will want to get up close and personal. So, I think he'll come after me the same way he came after Bill: in the privacy of my home. And, I'll be ready."

"George, this is just fucking nuts."

LITTLETON, CO
April 20
Two male students, aged 17 and 18, started shooting people at Columbine High School after the two propane bombs they left in the school cafeteria failed to explode. They killed 12 students and a teacher before committing suicide. It was the nation's worst school shooting at the time.

PHILADELPHIA, PA

April 21

Ennis awoke with Shoustal's fervent warning still resonating. After breakfast, he went to a gun shop on Spring Garden Street and bought a .45 caliber automatic and five boxes of cartridges. He then scheduled instruction on its use at a gun range near Pennsauken, N.J. (After two weeks that included the initial instruction and four practice sessions on the range, Ennis was comfortable with the gun and had become accurate enough to win praise from his instructor. He felt he was ready.)

April 22

"Have you ever once, over the last 30 years, considered getting married again or even living with someone?" Lansky asked Ennis. "I mean, now that I'm divorced again, I feel rather lonely at times. Don't you ever feel lonely?"

"Not really," Ennis responded. "I've grown rather fond of spending quality time with myself."

"Well, at least you said 'myself' instead of 'my favorite journalist.'"

"I wouldn't say that, Saul, because you're my favorite journalist—at least until you start typing."

Lansky smiled and said, "I must endure this kind of abuse from a middle-aged gigolo who titillates geriatric heiresses."

"I have intercourse with pre-geriatric waitresses, too," Ennis replied. "I'm an equal opportunity satyr, a shtupmeister for all demographics."

"In other words, you'll fuck anything that moves."

"Somethin' like that."

April 23

The dinner at the posh Union League was a tribute to slain Philadelphia policeman Daniel Faulkner, whose convicted killer, Mumia Abu-Jamal, had been on death row proclaiming his martyrdom

138

to a growing, worldwide following since his 1982 trial. Organized by radio talk show host Michael Smerconish, an attorney who had previously represented the Fraternal Order of Police in court, the tribute doubled as a fund-raiser to combat the Abu-Jamal camp's contentions that he had been treated unjustly by the Philadelphia justice system.

The 800 attending the tribute included Police Commissioner John F. Timoney, U.S. Senator Arlen Specter, Attorney General Mike Fisher, District Attorney Lynne Abraham, and Auditor General Robert Casey, Jr.

Mayor Ed Rendell, who was the district attorney when Abu-Jamal was tried, said the death row celebrity's supporters just wouldn't face the facts. The *Inquirer*'s Robert Moran reported the mayor saying: 'There are hundreds of people on death row in Pennsylvania who have been convicted with less overwhelming evidence than Mumia, but they just don't write poems and (actor) Ed Asner doesn't support them.'"

("Good old Fast Eddy," Lansky would say later. "You can always count on him for good copy.")

April 27
Ennis was sitting in his living room, going through an envelope full of photographs from his and Penelope's trip to Paris light years ago. There was a shot of Penelope on the tiny balcony of their cheap hotel, looking back at the camera with an impossibly sweet and sexy smile. The effect was to evoke lines from his favorite Dolly Parton song, the title piece from her 1977 album, *Here You Come Again.*

"Here you come again lookin' better than a body has a right to/An' shakin' me up so that all I really know/Is here you come again an' here I go."

April 30
The Vietnam War ended with the fall of Saigon on April 30, 1975. Ennis had been assigned to come up with some interesting facts about

the war for a piece marking the 24th anniversary of its conclusion. Here is part of what he found:

—The percentage of U.S. volunteers in Vietnam, a less than popular war, was higher than in World War II. And so was the number of deserters. In fact, more American military personnel deserted during the Vietnam War than during any other war in U.S. history. The Department of Defense reported 503,926 deserters between July 1, 1966, and December 31,1973. There were about 50,000 during World War II, and 13,790 during the Korean War. The majority of desertions during the Vietnam War took place in the U.S. and were usually by troops who had returned from a tour of duty.

—The average age of a U.S. infantryman was 22, but 11,465 were teenagers.

—During World War II, the average infantryman in the South Pacific saw 40 days of combat in four years. In Vietnam, thanks to the mobility afforded by the helicopter, the average soldier was in battle for 240 days in a single year!

—In all, 900,000 injured U.S. soldiers were airlifted to hospitals during the war. Though many lives were saved by helicopters rapidly transporting the grievously wounded to state-of-the-art hospitals, there was a grisly corollary: the number of survivors left with amputations and crippling wounds was 300 percent higher than it was during World War II.

May 5 and 6

Ennis had a dozen copies made of each of the three Dietrich sex pictures and took them to work. He was on the last shift—the lobster shift—which ended at 3:00 a.m. on the sixth. He went into the lavatory at quitting time and waited until the newsroom emptied. Then he pinned three incest shots on the bulletin board near the city desk and slipped three more under the door of the paper's editor, Gerard Henderson. The rest were placed on the desks of editors and rewrite men.

Later that morning, at 10:15 a.m., Henderson's secretary called Dietrich and told him the *Public Sentinel's* editor wanted to see him immediately.

"What's this about?" Dietrich asked.

"He didn't say."

A hush settled over the newsroom as Dietrich walked through it en route to Henderson's office. People stopped talking and typing. They stared at him, some incredulously, some with disgust.

At this point, Dietrich was pretty sure what had happened.

Henderson's secretary, stationed in an anteroom outside his office, walked through the editor's open door and announced Dietrich's arrival. The 6-5 columnist loomed in the doorway, his shiny scalp just three inches from the top of the door frame. Henderson motioned to a chair in front of his desk.

"This is why I asked you here," he said, fanning out the three sex pictures on the desk. "Dozens of these photographs showed up in the newsroom today. What do you have to say for yourself?"

"Does it matter? I mean, you're going to fire me anyway, aren't you? So, why should I grovel, why should I stoop?"

"Sign this," Henderson said then, shoving a one-sentence letter of resignation across the desk.

Dietrich glanced at the nine-word death sentence for a career and signed it. On his way out, he turned in the doorway and said: "I'll be comfortable in retirement, and I won't have to waste any more time suffering bourgeois clowns like you."

"Get the hell out of here, before I call security," Henderson said.

Dietrich had no more trouble discerning the source of those familiar photos than he did identifying the person who took them years earlier. It had to be Guest's old buddy (his only buddy as far as Dietrich could recall), George Ennis. Normally, Dietrich wouldn't have allowed emotions to affect his wet work. You don't mix personal matters with business. But then again, this wasn't business, it was personal. The man had disgraced him and ended his career. So, he would make Ennis pay, exacting a hot vengeance he would temper with professional cool.

But first things first. He closed the last of his four U.S. bank accounts. (He had emptied the first three after the police questioned him.) As he did with the others he closed, he arranged to deposit the proceeds in banks in Switzerland and the Cayman Islands. Next, he cashed out his mutual funds, put some of that money aside for expenses, and transferred the rest to his numbered Swiss account.

In all, his overseas nest eggs would amount to $1,100,000 ($2,032,220 in current dollars), which would be augmented by the proceeds from the sale of his expensive home, which he owned free and clear. He authorized his attorney to sell the home in his absence, then arranged to ship his favorite furnishings and vintage Ferrari to Europe where he would keep them in storage while he traveled around the south of France looking for a place to live.

With all that accomplished, he was ready to take care of his unfinished business with Ennis, a prospect that prompted a perversion of a great Dylan Thomas poem, "Do not go gentle into that good night.".

"He will not go gentle into that good night," Dietrich vowed, leaning back in his Le Corbusier chair with a glass of 12-year-old burgundy. "He 'will rage, rage against the dying of the light.'"

While Dietrich was getting his affairs in order, Ennis was getting his defenses in order.

Ennis now lived in Philadelphia's Queen Village, in a 19th-century house called a "trinity" (a small, three-story rowhouse with one room on each floor). The showdown that he anticipated here was based on several assumptions.

As he had mentioned to Shoustal, he felt Dietrich would try to take him out in his home. And since the house had security bars on the first-floor windows, and a lock and draw bolt on the rear door, he reasoned that while he was away, Dietrich would pick the lock on the front door and then lie in wait for him—probably behind the sofa in the first-floor living room.

The response he planned would begin with an old trick: When leaving the house, he would connect the bottom of the front door to the threshold with a nearly invisible piece of fine fishing line leader held in place by tiny pieces of clear tape. If the door was opened, it would pull the leader loose and indicate entrance.

When returning to the house, Ennis would be carrying the .45 he kept in his car when he left home. If he found the leader filament torn loose, he would execute a precise entry plan. After chambering the first round, he would take a position next to the door and open it. Next, he would flick the switch for the living room light he'd had installed just inside the door, then drop down and come across the short foyer on his belly with the gun aimed at the sofa on the opposite wall. If Dietrich presented himself, he would shoot him.

May 7

Like the rest of her Main Line home, Charlotte's bedroom was expansive and densely populated with exquisite antiques. The latter included an ornate bed that dated from the time of Louis the 14th, on which she and Ennis were reclining in the wake of sex.

Presently, Ennis rolled over and began moving his hand slowly up the inside of her right thigh.

"I'm a little sore, George. Maybe one roll in the hay is enough for a 1936 vintage."

"How sad," Ennis said. "Fine wines argue for a second glass."

She smiled. "I've really grown quite fond of you," George. "You started out as a decorative playmate, but you've graduated into something more."

"Gee, I've been promoted from fuck private to gigolo first class." replied an unsmiling Ennis. "Now, that's upward mobility for you."

"George, I simply wanted to say that my feelings for you have changed. They are deeper, more complex now. I certainly didn't want to offend you."

"Well, that was the effect."

"I'm sorry for that, I really am. But, I must say, you are being a tad touchy, maybe even a little class conscious."

"Of course I'm class conscious. You're Main Line old money and I grew up on a small farm in upstate New York."

Charlotte was getting annoyed. "Is my so-called 'promotion' of you that much different from the way you promoted your late wife from casual sex partner to love interest?"

"First of all, I resent having my dead wife drawn into this conversation. Secondly, I think that falling in love with someone and wanting to marry that person is a little different from what you have in mind for me."

"I'm getting a little tired of apologizing, George. Let's talk about something else. How 'bout a little getaway? We could fly to Cannes and stay at my villa. The film festival starts in a week. We could catch that. You do enjoy the festival, don't you?"

"I wouldn't know, I've never attended it."

Incredulity made her squint. "You've never been to the Cannes Film Festival? But, you're an entertainment writer!"

"The paper just sends our film critic."

"Can you stay for dinner?" she asked.

"Thanks, but I have to be at work in an hour."

"Then, come over tomorrow for lunch. Maybe we can resume our getaway discussion and frolic a bit."

"Okay."

May 7

Ennis finished his 5:00 p.m. to 1:00 a.m. shift and drove down to the Quill & Scroll. There, he struck up a conversation with one Pauline Schell, a 49-year-old freelance photographer who took him home.

He got back to his apartment at 10:35 Saturday morning. The phone rang as he opened the door. It was Lansky.

"I can't," Ennis said." I told Charlotte I'd come over for lunch."

"Does that mean what I think it means?"

"Yep, more wear and tear on a sex organ still recovering from last night and yesterday afternoon. You know, I think I'm getting too old for carnal triathlons. The spirit is still willing, but the flesh not so much.

"George, I'm so afraid your fatigue will result in a serious fall. I'll be right over with an aluminum walker."

"What I need is an aluminum dick."

"Well," Lansky responded, "welcome to the aging process, my man. No one ever said nocturnal emissions were forever."

Later that day, contemplating the complexity of his sex life, Ennis leaned back on his sofa, managed a small smile, and inserted a CD in the player. "Take It Easy," an Eagles hit released in 1972, came to life.

"Well I'm runnin' down the road tryin' to loosen my load/I've got seven women on my mind/Four that wanna own me, two that wanna stone me, one says she's a friend of mine/Take it easy . . ."

May 8

Ennis awoke suddenly, drew himself up to a sitting position, and confronted the vivid recollection of something at once familiar and frightening. In the weeks after he decided on the showdown, Ennis had experienced a recurring dream featuring a Civil War battle scene. In it, his great-grandfather, a teenage corporal in the Union cavalry, finds himself at the battle of Cold Harbor, perhaps the war's most vivid glimpse of hell.

Muzzle fire had ignited the dry forest where the battle took place. The satanic heat and choking smoke were everywhere. Flames advanced on downed soldiers too badly wounded to do anything but scream. Ennis's great-grandfather, Roger Ennis, Company H, Fifth Regiment, Pennsylvania Cavalry, had just had his horse shot out from under him. As he pulled himself to his feet, a Confederate infantryman rushed out of the smoke and fire, coming at him with a fixed bayonet.

Cpl. Ennis drew his cavalry saber and sidestepped the onrushing

145

Reb. As the Confederate stopped and wheeled, Ennis, both hands on the hilt, drove his sword into the young man's abdomen, near the navel. The Confederate landed on his back. His eyelids fluttered as blood and a gurgling sound issued from his mouth. He died seconds later.

Cpl. Ennis swallowed, then pulled the curved blade from the dead man's gut. This act was accompanied by a realization as stunning as it was Arthurian. The corporal's searing revelation (it was not clear in the dream whether it was spoken or thought) was that "He who withdraws this Northern blade from these Southern bowels shall rule over his own kingdom of hell."

Later, Ennis worked his shift and drove home. It was 8:20 p.m. when he parked. As usual, he took the gun from under the seat and headed for the front door. Glancing down at the base of the door, he saw that the clear tape attaching the leader to the threshold was pulled loose. He figured Dietrich was probably inside, waiting for him behind the sofa.

Ennis chambered a round, then positioned himself by the door and reached for his keys. But he froze as he was about to place the key in the lock. The inaction lasted 10 seconds. He then returned the keys to his pocket and went back to his car where he put the gun back under the front seat and called the Philadelphia police on his cell phone. A female dispatcher answered in a monotone.

"My name is George Ennis. I live at Catharine Street in Queen Village. I believe someone is inside my house.

"No, I'm not there. I'm in my car at Second and Catharine. I'll meet the policemen there and tell them what I think is going on."

Two patrolmen arrived in a squad car five minutes later. Ennis identified himself and showed them his press credentials so they'd be less likely to think him a nut case when he told them that Homicide was investigating the man he thought was inside. He also opined that Dietrich was probably there to kill him for posting pictures in the newsroom of him having sex with his sister.

"This guy is a hitman, a professional," Ennis said, handing his keys to one of the officers. "If he's in there, he's armed!

"There are bars on all the first-floor windows and the back door has a deadbolt and a second lock that can only be opened with the key," he added. "So, the front door is his only way out."

He and the policemen walked to the house. He hung back while the patrolmen took up positions on either side of the door. One of them called out: "Police, open up!"

When there was no response, the policeman unlocked the front door, stepped to the side, swung it open, and yelled: "Come out with your hands up!"

As he trained his .38 caliber revolver on the interior darkness, the other patrolman traversed it with his flashlight.

Seeing nothing, the patrolman with the flashlight stepped inside and turned on the overhead light in the living room.

Upstairs, Dietrich found himself terrified by the prospect of getting caught.

The two had barely completed their perusal of the living room when they heard the screech of a tight wooden window sash on the street side of the second floor.

"I'll go up there," said the patrolman with the light. "You take the street."

By the time his partner had reached the sidewalk, Dietrich had already jumped—and broken his right leg in the process.

The compound fracture had him writhing on the pavement as the policeman approached.

"Keep your hands where I can see them," the cop said, lowering his gun. "Now, roll on your side and put 'em behind your back."

"My leg's broken. The pain is excruciating!" Dietrich protested.

"I don't give a country fuck," the policeman said. "Roll over and put 'em behind your back!"

Dietrich obliged. The patrolman holstered his gun and cuffed him.

The other patrolman had arrived by this time. "Hey Bozo, aren't you getting a little long in the tooth to be doing a Peter Pan out a second-story window?" he asked as he patted Dietrich down.

"Hey, what've we got here?" he added, extracting a .22 caliber revolver from one of Dietrich's jacket pockets.

Ennis joined the trio and said to the policemen: "It'll be interesting to see if ballistics can match this gun to the one that killed my friend."

Dietrich was taken to the hospital to have the leg fracture treated, then placed in a cell at the district station while one of the police lab's ballistics experts checked his gun against the rifling marks on one of the bullets that struck Guest.

May 9

Ennis and Lansky were sitting at the dining room table in Lansky's townhouse in the city's Fairmount section, playing poker and consuming beer and stale soft pretzels.

"Boy, we bachelors really know how to live, don't we?" Lansky observed, his teeth eliciting a crunch from a pretzel that was not supposed to crunch. His small smile dissipated and he allowed that Dietrich obviously had figured out that Ennis was the source of the incest shots. (Ennis had told him about finding the prints and research, giving them to the police, and keeping several pictures that he eventually distributed in the newsroom.)

"Oh, sure. Like everybody else at the paper back then, he knew Bill and I were close friends."

"Well, you were taking a big chance then. You put yourself in harm's way first to try to get him arrested, and then to disgrace him."

"I'm going to tell you something that must remain between us," Ennis said. "I wasn't just trying to disgrace him with those pictures I spread around the newsroom. I was trying to flush him out, goad him into coming after me."

"George, that was crazy."

"I know, but he killed a dear friend and god knows how many others, and it looked like he was going to skate. I was infuriated and swore to myself that I would get him. I went out and bought a gun and learned how to use it. I figured he'd come after me in my home like he did with Bill, so I rigged the door each morning when I left so I'd know if anyone had entered in my absence.

"If I found the door had been opened, I would come in low with my gun ready. If I got him, I would have shot an intruder. End of story.

"But when push came to shove, I just couldn't do it. I couldn't bring myself to try to kill someone, even someone that monstrous. And, truth be told, I wasn't too keen on the flip side: the possibility of being killed by him.

"So, I wimped out and called the police. And in the end, I wasn't an avenging vigilante. I was just your standard, garden variety pussy."

"What you did was about humanity and common sense, not cowardice," Lansky concluded.

May 10
Ennis walked into Infante's office at 10:00 a.m. this Monday morning.

"Thank you for seeing me," Ennis said. "Have you learned anything?"

"Since the bullet that passed through Guest's chest exited his body virtually unscathed, the lab was able to get a conclusive ballistics match. This is the same gun that killed Guest.

"We're seeking a warrant to search his home for the .45 Guest mentioned in his findings," Infante continued. "If we can find that gun, and tie it to some of his other hits, it's a slam dunk. But even if we can't, we still have the gun used in Guest's death in his possession, and when you factor in Dietrich's visit to your place and the fact that that can be tied to Guest's photos and research, I think we'd still be in business on a murder charge. At the very least, we'll get him some jail time for breaking and entering, carrying a concealed weapon, and trying to flee from the police at a crime scene."

By noon, Homicide had obtained a warrant to search Dietrich's home. Three crime lab technicians moved methodically from room to room looking in, under, and behind every piece of furniture in the house. The interior spaces were measured, then compared with the corresponding exterior dimensions.

After four hours of careful searching, nothing had turned up in the living areas, basement, garage, or attic. The technicians were about to call it a day when one of them gave out a whoop from a guest bedroom on the second floor.

"Look at this!" he exclaimed when his colleagues entered the room. He pointed to the south side of the room where a closet was flanked by two walls flush with its doorway.

"This back closet wall is also the south wall of the house. Since the closet is 34 inches deep, that means there are 34-inch dead spaces behind each of its flush sides. Let's get the clothes out of here and see if we can find some access."

The three men carefully examined the interior of the cedar-lined closet. The technician who had discovered the apparent dead space noticed something on the closet's left-side wall: a slight gap between the cedar wall and the baseboard. The baseboard seemed a little springy, not solidly attached to the wall. He pulled on the top edge of the baseboard with his fingertips and it turned out to be a hinged panel that folded out to reveal a handle. He turned the handle—and the wall became a door to the dead space.

The technician's flashlight revealed a light switch, which, in turn, illuminated the tools of Dietrich's trade hanging in neat rows on the wall. There was a Bowie knife, binoculars, a Remington bolt-action 30-06 hunting rifle with a telescopic sight, a Winchester lever-action 30-30 deer rifle with open sights, 13 boxes of ammunition, a German 8mm Mauser bolt-action rifle of Second World War vintage, and a .45 automatic, also WWII issue.

A smile of accomplishment spread like a brush fire over the face of the technician who made the discovery. "If this is the .45 that Homicide is hoping it is, we hit the mother lode!" he said. "And I will insist that Infante owes me dinner at Le Bec-Fin."

May 11

The Philadelphia police crime lab had asked the police departments that investigated the murders Guest had mentioned in his report to send along the .45 caliber slugs recovered from the crime scenes. Twenty-seven bullets came in from 11 crime scenes. Of those slugs, 13 were sufficiently intact to permit ballistic comparisons with Dietrich's .45. By late afternoon, the crime lab technicians were able to conclusively connect the columnist's weapon to four more murders, including the 1969 killings of United Motors chairman Kenneth Briggs and his wife, the 1967 murder of a Tucson, Arizona, real estate developer named Eli Nussbaum, and the 1968 assassination of Clinton Burwell, an Atlanta auto parts manufacturer.

So, early this Tuesday evening, the already incarcerated Dietrich was charged with four more murders. Later, Homicide's Infante picked up his phone and dialed Ennis at his desk.

"We just charged Dietrich with four more counts of murder," he told Ennis. "Ballistics tied his .45 to those deaths. And the expense accounts show he was in those cities when the shootings took place. So, between that and the ballistics match in the Guest murder, we got this dick wad well and truly by the short hairs."

"Any chance he'll be granted bail?" Ennis wondered.

"No, he's not going to get bail. Even if the charge were less than murder one, he wouldn't get it. He's moved his money offshore and put his house up for sale. He's an obvious flight risk.

"I might add that this isn't just a local murder case anymore. Since he crossed state lines to commit four of those killings, the feds get into the act."

The charges against the disgraced columnist comprised the lead story on the 11 o'clock evening news.

Clinton J. Burwell, Jr., 49, switched off the Channel 6 newscast he was watching in the living room of his home in Chadds Ford, Pa., and walked into the kitchen where his wife was breading flounder fillets for dinner. The alarm in his face was contagious.

"My god, Clint, you look like you've seen a ghost!"

"They got the bastard who killed my father," Burwell said. "He was a sportswriter for the *Public Sentinel* until recently. He also moonlighted as a hitman, according to the police."

"Who would want to have your father killed?" his wife asked.

"I have a pretty good idea. I remember my dad seeming quite distracted in the days leading up to his death. I also heard him on the phone saying: 'You aren't going to get away with this!' I think he was talking to his partner, Jason Bellamy. Bellamy was a compulsive gambler who took what we thought was a healthy business into bankruptcy not too long after dad died. I think dad caught him with his hand in the till and was going to dime him out—and Bellamy had him killed before he could. But we'll probably never know, seeing as Bellamy died in a car crash five months after dad's death."

May 13

Ennis and Lansky were having dinner in the *Public Sentinel*'s cafeteria. Lansky said:

"You notice that new copy editor in features, Regina Dowd? Mid-20s. A real cutey."

"What I notice about women that age is that they really don't notice me," Ennis said. "It's funny. You get accustomed earlier in life to young women taking an interest, and then, one day, it's like they don't even see you. They seem to look right through you, like you're invisible. I know it's the way of the world and all that, but it still stings the first time you feel irrelevant to young women.

"Happily, what coincided with that awareness was a gathering appreciation of my peers. I've found that I really like the company of middle-aged women. They've lived long enough to be interesting, and they have a certain worldliness about them that I find quite sexy."

"Does that mean you'd turn your back on an opportunity to frolic with a 21-year-old *Playboy* centerfold?" Lansky asked.

"I wouldn't kick her out of bed on a cold winter's night, but I wouldn't seek her continued company, either. I mean, dating a kid is really a variation on the trophy wife, isn't it? And while that's an ego trip for a lot of men, I would find it humiliating."

"Humiliating?"

"Well, yeah. People looking at you and thinking: Boy, that old fuck must have money. Why else would she bother with him?"

Lansky smiled and said: "I was struck by you saying you wouldn't seek the centerfold's continued company. Since when, in the last 30 years, have you sought any woman's continued company?"

"Touché."

May 14

Ennis had the top down on his Porsche 911. He and Lansky were hurtling down a rural road in the Philadelphia hinterland, headed for a party near Chadds Ford, site of a Revolutionary War battle and home to the painter Andrew Wyeth.

Lansky fidgeted. "George, can you ease up on the gas a little?"

"Speed's not a problem as long as you know the limits of the car and its driver and stay within them," Ennis responded.

"What if a deer jumped out as we rounded a corner?" Lansky wondered.

"Come on, Saul, you don't buy a 911 if you wanna drive it like you have a pussy where your dick should be."

"George, that's such macho bullshit and you know it. I realize a Porsche is a car that says, my dick is bigger than your dick, but I didn't know that not driving it dangerously suggests you have no dick at all."

Ennis downshifted for a hairpin corner and said: "Well, as I always say, if the pussy fits, wear it."

"Fuck you and the Porsche you rode in on."

Later, at the party, Ennis met a recently divorced lawyer named Diane Rohrbach. She was 51 with a lean, gym-carved body that included civil C-cup implants. She had a ready wit and smile, and Ennis found her appealing.

As it turned out, she was something of a fan.

"I've been reading you for years," she said. "I particularly liked the piece you did recently on James Earl Jones."

"I have a lot of respect for him," Ennis said. "He's a superb actor."

"So, what about the flip side? Who didn't you like?"

"Lauren Bacall, for one. She was probably the nastiest interview I've ever had as an entertainment writer. It was one of those deals where the show's producer got the name brand to agree, grudgingly, to do a certain number of encounters with the press proles. I met with her in the morning. She was sans makeup, looked every bit of her 53 years, and tore me a new asshole when I tried to bring up the Bogart era.

"But, enough of my dreary past, let's talk about a very attractive counselor," Ennis said, as they finished their third mixed drink.

She smiled. "Thank you. That's nice to hear, seeing as my ex-husband traded me in for a newer model."

"I can't imagine why any man would walk away from you," Ennis said.

She touched his cheek and said: "That's so sweet of you to say. I'm appreciative, even if you are just being nice."

"If I'm just being nice, why have I spent the last 10 minutes trying to hide an erection?"

"Mr. Ennis," she said with a quizzical smile, "I can't believe you said that. Am I blushing?"

"Happily, no. I'd hate to see vascular graffiti on that perfect porcelain."

She smiled. "Wow! That's quite a pivot: from outrageous to alliterative in the blink of an eye."

Ennis grinned. "It's getting kind of warm in here, thanks to you. Why don't we go out on the patio and cool off?"

Outside, he moved her to the side of the sliding glass door where they couldn't be seen from inside, placed his hands on her waist, and kissed her. He then let his hands drop to her ass, pulled her to him hard, and kissed her again.

"Is this your idea of cooling off?" she asked.

Ennis smiled. "Since tomorrow's weekend, perhaps I could take you to lunch," he said.

I'll make lunch for you," she replied, smiling impishly. "Say, around noon?"

Later, on the drive back to the city, Lansky said: "You've got that one treed, don't you?"

"Being a subtle sophisticate, no doubt worthy of a place in the court of The Sun King, I wouldn't put it that crassly. But it is true that Diane of Avondale has requested my presence at a noon luncheon in the solarium of her country residence."

"Gee, I can't imagine what the first course will be," Lansky said.

May 15

Ennis pulled onto the macadam driveway leading to Diane Rohrbach's Avondale home, a glass and redwood-enclosed contemporary on three wooded acres.

He flicked the ignition key, causing the 911's six pistons and connecting rods to stop thrashing. He walked to the front door and knocked. She answered the door in a perfectly tailored white knit cocktail dress.

Ennis put his hands on her waist and kissed her.

"I love your dress," he said. "Of course, you'd be exquisitely distracting in a burlap bag."

"Thank you, kind sir," she said, smiling. "Flattery of that caliber will gain you access to my most secret sites."

He kissed her again and ran his hands over her ass.

"Don't you want to eat first?" she asked.

"Perhaps we could preface the meal with an *amuse-bouche*," he replied.

"I never understood what was amusing about appetizers," Diane said.

"Chef George's Michelin marvels are many things," Ennis replied, "but I hope they aren't amusing."

They emerged from the bedroom 40 minutes later. She was now wearing a dressing gown and smudged makeup.

"I'm a bit disheveled," she observed.

"You look wonderful," Ennis assured her.

Lunch was served in the solarium and consisted of vichyssoise followed by cold salmon on a bed of vinaigrette-anointed arugula.

Ennis refilled her glass from the bottle of Santa Margherita pinot grigio he had brought along.

"I figure if I ply you with a little more wine, I might be able to take advantage of you."

I don't remember my inhibitions being an impediment to your advances during our alcohol-free amuse-bouche."

They moved from the table to a love seat. Ennis sat by her, parted her gown, and then knelt on the floor between her legs. Her subsequent orgasm was rather violent.

"Now, that's a world-class scratch," Ennis observed, eyeing his bleeding right bicep. "I thought you brides of Dracula employed overgrown incisors to draw blood."

"I'm not a bride of Dracula," Diane responded. "We're divorced. Anyway, I'm sorry. Here, let me kiss your grievous wound and make it better."

"Absolutely not! The taste of blood could inspire you to visit one of my carotid arteries, and I don't want to have to quit my day job and sleep in a casket."

She ran her hand up his thigh. "Could I kiss you somewhere else if I promise not to bite," she said.

Two hours and several genital interactions later, Ennis buttoned his shirt and pulled on his pants.

"Ever tried a ménage à trois?" Diane asked.

"Once."

"How'd you like it?"

"Well, something I had always fantasized about turned out to be decidedly underwhelming. The better-looking woman sucked and fucked me while her hefty friend with the flaccid breasts lay naked beside us, talking on the phone to her married boyfriend, the firemen. After the cuter one and I got off, the heifer hung up, crawled on top of me, and made a brief, half-hearted effort to resurrect my limp dick. It was almost as if she didn't want to cheat on her married boyfriend.

"Maybe," he concluded, "if both women had gotten it on with me and with each other—you know, a real triple play—it might have been different."

"My friend, Cynthia, and I would be happy to play mix-and-match with you," Diane said.

Ennis squinted at her. "Never took you for a switch hitter," he said.

"Since college. My ex never knew."

"Probably just as well. So, what's Cynthia like?"

"She's 47, and a colleague of mine. And other than the fact she's witty, very pretty, and has a body that will leave your penis in full bloom, she's utterly forgettable."

"You've sold me, counselor. Where do I sign?"

"Can you make it next Saturday, say around lunchtime?"

"I'll be there, my beautifully bodied barrister."

"George, you shouldn't be so alliterative. It makes me wet."

May 17

"So, you're really going to 'ménage it' with two cuties?" Lansky said as he and Ennis entered the *Public Sentinel*'s lobby.

"Yessir," Ennis replied. "My research into the nature of the human condition is without boundary."

"Blow it out your ass, you goofy goyim," a grinning Lansky responded.

"Goofy goyim? One cannot speak like that around Diane," Ennis

157

said, as he pressed the elevator button. "She told me alliteration leaves her quite aroused.

"Seriously, I do like Diane. I wouldn't go so far as to say I've had monogamous thoughts about her, but I do enjoy her company and she is an ace in the sack."

The elevator door opened onto the newsroom, where the two were confronted by a gaggle of sheet-draped, four-foot-high figures with papier-mâché faces and placards hung from their necks identifying them in ways that only the newsroom cognoscenti would grasp. For example, the sign on one figure, which represented a mild-mannered but quite political deputy editor, referred to him as "the killer choir boy."

The assemblage, surreptitiously installed over the weekend, was the work of Ken Bowers, a moody idealist given to satirizing the newsroom's high priests.

After Bowers' handiwork had elicited a succession of chuckles from the two men, Lansky turned to Ennis: "I thought you said this new newsroom breed was such a boring bunch?"

"I certainly erred in this guy's case," Ennis said.

"You did, and an appropriate punishment is in order for your judgmental generalizations," Lansky replied. "I was thinking of locking you in a dark room where you would be forced to spend an entire evening listening to recordings of Arnold Schwarzenegger speaking the English language."

Jon Mecklinburg, the *Public Sentinel* editor who replaced Grimsley when he retired, unobtrusively joined the two men surveying the Bowers installation. He smiled thinly and said, "I had no idea this kind of shit was rolling around in that man's head."

May 22

Ennis knocked, and Diane Rohrbach answered her door. She ushered him into the living room, where Cynthia Freeman rose to greet him. She was about 5-8, a statuesque beauty with a topography that was quite womanly but didn't enlist enough female fat to get her modeling work in the studios of ancient Greek sculptors and Renaissance painters. (Ennis decided her bra size dwelled in the beguiling border country between B and C.) She had hair as black and shiny as anthracite, green eyes, flawless skin, and lovely facial bone structure.

"You're as gorgeous as Diane said you were," Ennis observed. "The question is, can you cook?"

"I've mastered the microwaving of frozen macaroni and cheese dinners," she replied through a smile, "That's my culinary high water mark."

"Perhaps there's some extra credit work you can do in the bedroom to bring your grade average up," Ennis said.

Diane ushered her guests into her large, airy bedroom which included a king-sized bed. She kissed Ennis and rubbed his genitals through his jeans.

"Being a gallant sort, I thought I might assist you ladies in shedding the raiment that provides hostages to fortune."

"Oh please, kind sir, free me from these hostages," Diane said.

Slowly, ceremoniously, Ennis removed her shoes, dress, bra, and finally her panties. He then fondled her ass and kissed her lips and nipples before moving on to Cynthia, who got the same treatment.

"Now, it's our turn," Cynthia said, and the two proceeded to strip him. Diane then squeezed his balls while Cynthia stroked his dick.

"Now, I'd like to do something for you," the rampant Ennis said. He then seated them side by side on the edge of the bed, had them lie back, and then alternately committed cunnilingus on one while fingering the other. Diane came first. Cynthia quickly followed suit.

"May I suggest a follow-up?" Ennis asked.

"Please do," Cynthia responded.

"How 'bout if Diane gets down on her knees and then gets down on you while I kneel behind her and file a motion from there?"

"How can we deny a man with such a command of lawyerly locutions?" Cynthia wondered.

159

"We can't," Diane replied as her face neared Cynthia's labia.

After he came in Diane, he sucked on tits and clits until his middle-aged reproductive system had recharged enough to do Cynthia.

They had drinks and dinner after that, followed by Ennis eschewing a return to the bedroom for a postprandial finale.

"Thank you, ladies, for a marvelous sojourn, but I have to leave. I must take my aging genitals to the emergency ward."

"We'll visit if you have to be admitted," Cynthia said.

May 24

"So, how was the ménage?" Lansky asked Ennis.

"It was pretty good. But I think I'll try to see them separately the next time around. I guess I'm a monogamist in spirit."

"Yeah, right," Lansky said. "You're clearly a one-woman kind of guy."

June 1

Lansky and Ennis were both off at 10:00, but Lansky had to stay a little longer to finish a piece before he could join his friend at Freddie's.

"What are you drinking?" Lansky inquired, as he took a stool next to Ennis.

"It's a medication made from a healthful grain whose complex carbohydrates have been altered through distillation to enhance their germicidal properties," Ennis answered. "Sometimes, when called upon to perform emergency surgery in a non-medical setting, I pour it on open wounds."

"George, you don't know how profoundly sorry I am that I asked."

"Are you really going to put a move on that?" Ennis asked later, as he looked down the bar at a middle-aged blond. "I know we're getting old and it's getting late but, ah, that's something Oscar Wilde would have called 'a woman of repellant aspect.' If Woody Allen were here, he would describe her as having the body of a crab and the head of a social worker. I mean, I wouldn't fuck that with your dick."

Lansky took a drag on his pony bottle of Rolling Rock. "Beauty is in the eyes of the beer holder," he replied.

"Beauty is in the eyes of the beer holder? Saul, I didn't realize you spoke Bumper Sticker."

"Fucketh thou, vile goyim."

"Saul, you attack with such cruelty when I was about to compliment you?"

"About what?"

"I was about to say that housing authority story you were detached to report and write certainly shot holes in the official line on where that money was going. I think you have a pretty good detector."

"Detector?" Lansky responded.

"Yeah. Hemingway said that 'the most essential gift for a good writer is a built-in, shock-proof shit detector.' And that obviously goes for reporters as well as novelists."

June 24

"The guys who brought us along would hardly recognize the business now," Ennis said. "I mean, the old reporter/rewrite man tag team is almost extinct. We're just about all writing reporters now."

"Well, Jerry Eshelman and I still pull rewrite duty from time to time," Lansky said. "I guess we're about the only dinosaurs left."

"But you're the Michael Jordan of the dinosaurs," Ennis replied. "I kid you a lot, but you're one hell of a rewrite man. You're blindingly fast, which is why the editors still go to you when the shit hits the fan. I can't begin to write as fast as you can."

"And I can't begin to write as well as you," Lansky replied. "You've got some talent. I've often thought you ought to try your hand at a novel."

"I'm not an artiste, Saul. I'm a newspaperman. I don't write poetry in my spare time. I'm just a guy who tells stories to pay bills."

"You once told me you wrote poetry for your college's literary magazine," Lansky said. "And I remember when you submitted a short story to *The New Yorker*. So, you used to have dreams."

"I was a kid then. I'm 57 now. I'm too old to dream."

June 25

Ennis's Porsche was doing an effortless 85 on the early morning Schuylkill Expressway. When he turned the radio on, he found himself on an oldies station, listening to Roger Miller's 1969 rendition of Me and Bobby McGee (which he didn't enjoy as much as Janet Joplin's subsequent version). Like so many things in his life, it reminded him of Penelope, who really liked the Miller take on the song: "From the coal mines of Kentucky/To the California sun/Bobby shared the secrets of my soul . . . Then somewhere near Salinas, Lord/I let her slip away/Lookin' for that home I hope she'll find/And I'd trade all my tomorrows/For one single yesterday/Holdin' Bobby's body next to mine . . ."

Ennis blinked back tears, downshifted, and nailed the throttle. The 911's torque-rich, horizontally opposed six grew guttural and immediately added a digit to the speedometer reading.

June 30

Lansky and Ennis were in a bar on Germantown Avenue in Chestnut Hill.

"Who's that woman who keeps looking over at me?" Lansky asked.

"That's Ginny Mecum," Ennis replied. "She's a Republican ward leader. I understand she gives good head."

Lansky smiled. "I'm not interested in getting a blow job from somebody who sucks Republican dicks," he said.

"You're a man of principle, Saul, no question about it."

NEAR MARTHA'S VINEYARD, MA

July 16

A plane flown by John F. Kennedy, Jr. crashed here causing the death of the pilot, his wife, Carolyn Bessette Kennedy, and her sister, Lauren Bessette.

In its final report on the accident, the National Transportation Safety Board said the probable cause was "The pilot's failure to maintain control of the airplane during a descent over water at night, which was a result of spatial disorientation."

PHILADELPHIA, PA
July 20

Ennis and Lansky were sitting in Ennis's Porsche alongside a decrepit factory in South Philadelphia, eating big, meat-stuffed rolls from nearby John's Roast Pork, at Snyder and Weccacoe Avenues.

John's was as wonderful as it was grungy, simply because it manufactured the best Italian pork sandwiches in the city. (Ennis and Lansky always got theirs with sharp provolone.)

"You've been writing this showbiz shit now for more than 25 years," Lansky said between bites. "Still having any fun?"

"It has its moments, I guess, but it isn't as much of a kick as it was when I started back in the 70s. Still, it beats writing hard news on deadline or my stint in the features department doing the silly ass stories that come with that territory. John Cleese once rejoiced in life after Monty Python by telling an interviewer he didn't want to be 50 years old and still be dressing up like a chicken. Well, I wouldn't want to be my even more advanced age and still be driving up to Princeton to report on the latest campus fad."

"So, tell me about the rabbits, George. Which of the interviews was most memorable?"

Ennis was silent for a moment. "Certainly, the one with Peter Boyle was right up there. I talked to him when he was on the road promoting Mel Brooks's *Young Frankenstein*, in which he played the monster.

"Eventually, conversation turned to a previous Brooks film, *Blazing Saddles*. Boyle had no part in that movie but said he had hung around the set anyway, just because it was such fun watching it being filmed.

163

"He claimed the best line in that movie wound up on the cutting room floor. There's a scene where a horny Madeline Kahn is in a dark backroom with the black sheriff played by Cleavon Little and she says, 'It's twue, it's twue.' What they cut out, according to Boyle, was the sheriff's reply: 'Lady, that's my arm.'

"Another fun moment was an interview with two *Animal House* operatives: Harold Ramis, who helped write the film comedy, and Karen Allen, who had a role in it. Unlike some actresses, Karen wasn't a letdown in person. She was cute as a button.

"I asked Ramis about the scene in which Allen, who plays a student, appears bottomless after having sex at the home of a professor played by Donald Sutherland. Ramis turned to Allen, who was sitting next to him, and said: 'We wrote that scene because we all wanted to see Karen's ass.'

"She laughed.

"I also asked Ramis about the scenes where a fraternity asshole parks with his girl and then fails to get it up when she tries to jerk him off with a latex-gloved hand.

"So, why did you endow him with this sexual dysfunction?" I asked.

"Because we didn't like him," Ramis replied."

Ennis took a pull on his Pepsi and then said: "My encounter with Gilda Radner was a hoot, too. I interviewed her in a Manhattan rehearsal hall during a lunch break. We were sitting off to the side, and several of the other cast members kept inching closer to hear what she was saying.

"Finally, Gilda looked around and said, 'I feel like everyone's listening to me pee.'

"And my conversation with James Earl Jones was memorable. This was also back in the 70s, at a time when Broadway-bound shows did shakedown cruises in towns like Louisville, Washington, and Philadelphia before going on to New York. I went down to Louisville to see Jones's show and interview him for an advance on its Philadelphia performances.

"Jones proved delightful, a bright, pleasant man with something to say—a charge you can't level at a lot of actors. He came down to my hotel room with nearly a quarter of a bottle of whiskey. When he finished it, more than an hour into our conversation, he abruptly stood up, announced he had to meet someone, and left. That apparent use of a bottle of whiskey as an interview timer was a first for me.

"You know, I saw Jones years earlier in *The Great White Hope*. That was my first Broadway show, and I'll never forget it."

July 27

Ennis was headed down East River Drive toward Center City when Frank Sinatra's rendition of Laura came on the 911's radio. Beautiful and haunting, the song inevitably reminded Ennis of another haunting woman: "Laura is the face in the misty light/Footsteps that you hear down the hall/The laugh that floats on a summer night/That you can never quite recall/And you see Laura on a train that is passing through/Those eyes how familiar they seem/She gave your very first kiss to you/That was Laura but she's only a dream."

August 2

Ennis finished a feature for the Sunday entertainment section and walked over to Lansky's desk.

"Whatcha up to?" he asked, putting his hand on the shoulder of the seated Lansky.

"I'm doing some serious reporting for a significant news story, something you don't have to bother with in your role as a resident art-fart."

"Are you diminishing the majesty of my vocation?"

"And what would that vocation be, other than fucking actresses and then writing laudatory lies about them?"

"Geez, Saul, you aren't taking any prisoners today, are you? The fact is, I don't fuck actresses. Of course, that might not be true if they had any interest in fucking me. But alas, the blush of youth has left me and vaginas no longer dampen in my presence."

"If we're talking about vaginas of your vintage, they wouldn't dampen if you were Brad Pitt."

Ennis's lips formed a small smile and his eyes narrowed. "Speaking of aging, you're getting up there, Saul. You're 60, a sexagenarian. Isn't it about time you started thinking about retiring to Pigfuck, Florida?"

"Actually, I was leaning more toward Maconbacon, Georgia," Lansky replied.

"Saul, you will have to pay a price for making light of my advancing years and trivializing my artistic essence. I was prepared to treat you to a top-shelf martini at Freddie's. But now, you will get a Bud draft."

"My dear man," Lansky responded, "I am sufficiently capitalized to buy my own upmarket martini."

Ennis grinned broadly, replaced his hand on his friend's shoulder, and said: "Capitalized? I'm always surprised when you wax polysyllabic. Of course, I'm also surprised that you're bipedal."

"You know, Ennis, I ought to deck you for that. And I probably would if you weren't such an under-six-foot shrimp."

"Saul, I'm 5-11. That makes me one inch shorter than you."

"I bet you're 5-11. I never met a man under six feet who told the truth about his height."

August 15

Ennis was reading a nostalgic feature in the *Public Sentinel* reminding him that this was the 30th anniversary of the opening of the Woodstock Festival, those fabled four days when as many as a half-million young people gathered on a muddy upstate New York farm to get their fill of sex, drugs, and name brand rock and folk music.

He put the paper down, turned to the man at the next desk, and said: "You know, Saul, you and I are among five middle aged people in North America who have freely admitted to not being at Woodstock. The other three are either dead or in the Witness Protection Program."

"Yeah," Lansky responded, "even a plastic pocket protector type like Levandowski claimed he was there."

"Did he really?" Ennis asked. "And did he really seek safety from ballpoint pen leakage by wearing a plastic pocket prophylactic? I knew he was wifty. I guess I never noticed his nerd quotient."

"Well," Lansky said, "let's put it this way: He got a briefcase for his fifth birthday—and he liked it."

August 20

The trial of Horst Dietrich finally came to an end. It had lasted eight days and included the testimony of two ballistics experts who connected Dietrich's guns to the killings. Also testifying was a Tucson man who had told that city's police 30 years earlier that he had seen a very tall man running across Nussbaum's lawn on the night of the developer's murder and got a good look at him when he subsequently passed under a streetlight. A police artist's sketch from his description yielded nothing at the time, but in court, he identified Dietrich as that man.

The jury of seven women and five men deliberated just four hours before finding him guilty of first-degree murder. They then asked for the death penalty. The Dietrich verdict was the lead story on the 6 o'clock newscast. When the report was over, Burwell slumped back in his recliner and stared vacantly at the ceiling.

"Don't you at least feel some relief and satisfaction knowing that justice has finally been served and this animal will pay the ultimate price for what he did?" his wife asked.

"Will he?" responded Burwell, a partner at Kurtz & Stern, a Center City law firm. "He's already 61. He may well die of natural causes before he exhausts his appeals."

August 23

His desk phone rang and Ennis answered.

"Hello."

"Hi, George, it's Charlotte."

"Haven't seen you in a while," Ennis responded. "I called you the other day. You never called back."

"I might as well just say it, George. I've been seeing someone else, and it's grown quite serious."

"Who is he?"

"Bob Fisker."

"As in Fisker Industries?"

"Yes."

"Well, guess he won't be as class conscious as I was. Seriously, we had some good times, and I wish you well. I must say I'm a little disappointed that the kiss-off wasn't administered in person."

"I was afraid it would be too stressful," she said.

"I think you made the right decision," he replied. "I certainly wouldn't want your increased heartbeat on my conscience.

"See you around," he added, before hanging up.

August 24

Ennis was sitting in the *Public Sentinel*'s cafeteria having supper with Clint Winters, the newsroom's liaison with the paper's bean counters. Ennis looked up from his hamburger, which was identified by the chalkboard menu as "Salisbury Steak" because it was covered with gravy instead of a roll, and said to Winters: "The mood in the newsroom seems to become more funereal by the day. The drop in circulation has bred buyout rumors, and people know a diminished staff means diminished editorial quality, which, in turn, would suggest more circulation losses. So tell me, what's going on? I mean, the decrease in profits isn't that big. Isn't the *Public Sentinel* still making a good buck?

"Yes, it is," Winters answered. "Its margins are still double-digit, and that's enough profit to make most CEOs come all over Monica Lewinsky's dress. But it's not making as much as it once was, and that slippage is not a temporary state of affairs, it's a trend.

"The thing is, the internet is biting us in the ass in several ways, and the bite wounds are just going to get deeper. As more people get their news electronically, instead of from us, circulation will keep going down. Obviously, a loss of circulation means lost newspaper sales revenues, and, more important, a reduction in the ad rates.

"But just as important, in my view, is the fact that people are starting to change the way they sell their stuff as well as the way they get their news. Folks are increasingly buying and selling online—eBay comes to mind. As a result, the internet keeps eating into our ad lineage, classified in particular, and classified advertising is a big newspaper's cash cow. It's a license to print money that has helped put a presentable face on the newspaper industry's rather grim top management, and now that revenue is going away."

"Why do you think management is so bad?" Ennis wondered.

"Shortsightedness, primarily. At the moment, they seem more interested in short-term profits than in trying to make an endangered species sustainable."

Ennis smiled ironically. "Gee, Clint, I wasn't suicidal before I talked to you, but now I'm not so sure. Seriously, it sort of makes me glad I'm nearing the end of my vocational journey and can get out of Dodge if I have to. I just feel for the less aged folk who will be too young to retire, too old to get another job, and wind up having to ride this horse 'til it drops."

October 5

Horst Dietrich was sentenced to death. He was temporarily jailed in Philadelphia, where he filed appeals and awaited transfer to a federal prison. He shared a cell with a huge man named Howard Wosniak. He had been a star NFL offensive lineman earlier in the decade. But then the anabolic steroids that had served him so well on the football field produced a 'roid rage that left his wife dead on their bedroom floor.

In prison, the lack of steroids had helped shave 30 pounds off his 285-pound frame. But regular weight training kept the 6-5 athlete a hard-bodied force to be reckoned with. There were some other big boys in the prison exercise yard, but none of them tugged on Superman's cape.

It was fairly dark in their cell when Wosniak said to Dietrich: "I'll give you a choice tonight, bitch. You can either blow me or take it up the ass."

October 27

The lean, balding man in the olive drab jumpsuit had positioned himself at the top of an abandoned quarry overlooking Far Meadow Penitentiary, a maximum-security prison nestled in a little valley six miles from Scranton. From this vantage point, he could look down on the prison's exercise yard, which was occupied by inmates daily from 1:00 to 3:00 p.m., weather permitting.

The rifle he extracted from its leather sleeping bag was a .308 caliber Winchester Model 70 fitted with a powerful telescopic sight. Long a favorite with hunters and police sharpshooters, it accepted a shell virtually identical to the 7.62 mm NATO round.

The rifleman hunkered down behind a boulder at the top of the quarry cliff which he used to steady the .308. None of the nearby leaves was stirring. An eerie dead calm prevailed. He peered at the prison through the telescopic sight and saw the U.S. flag near the entrance hanging limply. No need to make a windage adjustment, he concluded. At a range of 250 yards, however, he would have to aim high to compensate for the bullet's bow to gravity.

He found his quarry sitting at a picnic table, facing in his direction. He was reading *Gourmet* magazine—a rather punishing pastime for someone living on prison food. The rifleman chambered a cartridge and estimated the bullet's drop. He then placed the crosshairs on a spot above the bald target's hairline. He squeezed the trigger with the gentleness of a nursing mother.

The .308 caliber bullet entered Horst Dietrich's forehead relatively neatly but made a bit of a mess where it exited near the base of his skull. He died almost instantly.

The killer viewed his handiwork through the scope. "I got him, Dad," he said softly.

Then Clinton J. Burwell, Jr., Center City lawyer, little league coach, and 25-kill U.S. Army sniper in Vietnam, put the rifle back in its case and started toward the Jeep Wrangler that would take him down the steep, rocky trail to the two-lane macadam.

Later that day, Ennis was writing a feature on his computer when homicide detective Marshall Brisbane called from the *Public Sentinel*'s lobby.

"I'd like to see you for a moment," Brisbane said.

"Sure, come on up. I'm on the fifth floor."

Brisbane presently appeared by his desk. "I have to ask you where you were this afternoon when Horst Dietrich was killed."

"I was right here doing what I'm doing now. These folks sitting around me can attest to that."

Brisbane talked with three of Ennis's co-workers, who supported his story, then returned to Ennis's desk.

"It was a base we had to cover, George."

"I understand."

December 21

Ennis was in the paper's library, looking for local newsworthy nuggets to be published in a year's end roundup. Among them was the Man of the Year award bestowed by Harvard's Hasty Pudding Theatricals on Bill Cosby, a comedian, actor, and Philadelphia native. (Cosby went on to win dozens of honors ranging from a Yale honorary doctorate to the Presidential Medal of Freedom. More recently, in 2018, he was found guilty of three charges of aggravated indecent assault and subsequently imprisoned.)

December 23

Lansky grimaced slightly as he rubbed the small of his back.

"Well, George, it's just hell to get old," he said.

"Oh, I don't know," Ennis replied. "It's like Tennyson's aging Ulysses says: 'Though much is taken, much abides.' Hell, I can still bench press my body weight and my dick still gets hard. So, I really can't complain.

"I do miss Penelope, though."

"George, it's been 30 years of one-night stands, or what amount to one-night stands, 30 years of avoiding any real connections with women. Isn't it time to kiss Penelope goodbye and get on with your life?"

"She was the only woman I ever loved."

"I know that, George. But that doesn't mean you couldn't have a pleasant, even affectionate relationship with another woman at this point in your life."

Ennis nodded.

December 27

It had been bitter cold. Four inches of snow and sleet fell on Philadelphia on Christmas, followed by 15.5 inches of snow the next day. Now, a day later, Ennis made his morning coffee and sat in the leather chair by the living room window, looking out over the playground across the street where the wind had swept the snowfall into waves of cold meringue. He opened an ornate little silver box containing a lock of Penelope's sepia hair and carefully removed a half dozen strands.

"Penelope," he said quietly, "I'm going to try to stop treating women the way I did before I fell in love with you—and the way I have since your death. I'm going to try for a relationship, some small reflection of what we had. But that doesn't mean I love you any the less, or ever will."

He got up then, opened the window, and let the wind carry the strands of hair toward December's dreaming drifts.

Later that afternoon, he called Samantha Jamison, a divorced, 51-

year-old *Public Sentinel* copy editor. Ennis always liked her. She was attractive, affable, and easy to be around. And she took good care of his copy.

"Samantha?"

"Yes."

"Hi, this is George, George Ennis. How ya doin'?"

"Good. And you?"

"Fine."

There were several seconds of silence.

"So, what's up?" Samantha asked, finally.

"Well, I'd like to take you to dinner this evening if you aren't otherwise engaged."

That evening, Samantha looked up from her lobster bisque, harboring a small, mischievous grin that reminded Ennis of Penelope.

"So, tell me, George, how often has a woman ever told you she was otherwise engaged when you asked her out?"

Ennis could think of one occasion. It seemed like a lifetime ago when Penelope said that to him in the Quill & Scroll. In fact, it was several years after he had set a course from Troy to Philadelphia.

It was a time when the voyage was still young and pregnant with the promise of fair skies and following winds.

1999 EPILOGUE

DETROIT, MI

January 17, 2000

The wire story carried a Detroit dateline. It began: "In a grisly instance of déjà vu, the retired chairman of United Motors and his wife were found shot to death yesterday in their suburban home, the apparent victims of an intruder who stole antiques and valuable art.

"Each had been shot several times.

"County Detective Marvin Bell said the murders bore a resemblance to the deaths, some 30 years earlier, of Harvick's predecessor, Kenneth L. Briggs, and his wife, Marsha. Both couples were residents of Grosse Pointe Farms, both were gunned down in bed, and, in each case, the stolen property included old silverware and a Picasso pen-and-ink drawing.

"Despite the similarities of the crimes, the detective declared a copycat killing unlikely. He told reporters there were significant differences in the two crimes that he wouldn't disclose, and that copycats don't typically wait three decades to act."

Later that day, a Detroit police captain watched the report of the Harvick murders on the evening news. He had had an interesting telephone conversation with Horst Dietrich just a few days prior to his October 27 assassination in the exercise yard at Far Meadow Penitentiary.

Thanks to a prison official who was an old friend of the captain, he was able to offer Dietrich prison perks for telling him what he knew about some unsolved Detroit hits. In the course of this questioning, the policeman asked him who paid for the hit on Kenneth Briggs and his wife 30 years ago. Dietrich, on death row with nothing to lose, told him he had learned it was Harvick.

The Detroit police captain, Kenneth L. Briggs, Jr., smiled when the county detective told the TV reporters that the similarities between the Harvick and Briggs killings were almost certainly coincidental.

ABOUT THE AUTHOR

Al Haas was born in Philadelphia in 1939 and grew up in Mount Penn, a suburb of Reading, Pa.

At age 14, after police had ended a search for an old man who had wandered off, Haas took his Boy Scout patrol on a search of Neversink Mountain—and found him.

He later played high-school basketball (when it was still possible for someone a mere 6'2" to start at center).

He was educated in Reading at Albright College (class of 1961), where he majored in English for two years and then spent the next two as a History major. He also wrote poetry for the school literary magazine, and after class worked 40-hour weeks as a night janitor.

After college, he worked for two small newspapers before joining *The Philadelphia Inquirer* staff in 1965. He spent the rest of his career there, working as a rewrite man, a local columnist, a Sunday magazine writer, an entertainment writer, and, finally, as an automotive columnist.

When offered the auto job because he was known to be an unredeemed teenage car freak (he built a Cadillac-powered 1934 Ford hot rod), Haas responded: "Let me get this straight. You're going to let me play with cars and pay me, too?"

Sudden Death Overtime is his first novel.

www.ingramcontent.com/pod-product-compliance
Lightning Source LLC
Chambersburg PA
CBHW021104130626
46554CB00002B/523